BAD
COMPANY

by the same author

DUPE

BAD
COMPANY

Liza Cody

CHARLES SCRIBNER'S SONS • NEW YORK

Library of Congress Cataloging in Publication Data

Cody, Liza.
  Bad company.

  I. Title.
PR6053.0247B3   1982   823'.914   82-23145
ISBN 0-684-17760-9

1 3 5 7 9 11 13 15 17 19 F/C 20 18 16 14 12 10 8 6 4 2

Printed in the United States of America.

To Dot and Mouse

CHAPTER 1

A sulking grey sky hung about fifty feet over the rooftops, threatening but not yet drenching the North London street below. Anna drove slowly while she and Bernie inspected the area.

'No yellow lines,' Bernie approved, 'and no residents' permit either. That's a start.'

'What number?' Anna asked.

'Twenty-nine.'

But she had to drive well past the house before she could find a space to park. They walked back slowly under the dripping lime trees, Bernie humming quietly to himself and appearing to look at nothing.

'Ground-floor flat,' Bernie murmured as they passed the house. Anna glanced at it from behind him. Steps led up to a blue front door. The large windows of the old Victorian house were covered with net curtains. Unlike most of the other houses, there were no trees growing in the small front garden. It was paved and weedy, with a circular flower-bed in the centre sporting a single crooked rose-bush.

'Mildew,' Bernie said, without turning, and they walked on to the corner of Haverstock Hill.

'Two pubs, a restaurant and a greengrocer,' he went on, looking up and down the main road. 'We shouldn't do too bad.'

They walked back to the car and Anna drove Bernie home. There was no mildew on his roses. In fact, everything in and around the Schiller home looked valued. Even the dog had a glossy coat and behaved as if it had never heard a cross word in its life. Anna always marvelled that anyone could live at such peace with his surroundings.

'I'll pick up the Commer van and meet you there,' she suggested. 'I've got to get up early anyway. My car's going in for its MOT tomorrow.'

'All right.' Bernie eased his large shoulders out of the car. 'You could get back to Kensington High Street before six and pick up a camera. I'll use my own. We'll meet at seven-thirty tomorrow morning. That should give us plenty of time to check out any visitors who stayed the night.'

'OK. But Bernie, what sort of skinny does this bloke want us to get on Mrs Fourie?'

'I don't think he knows himself,' he said, fishing his front-door keys out of a capacious pocket. 'Some sort of evidence that her way of life is corrupting his daughter, I suppose. We'll see.'

Driving away, Anna felt vaguely irresponsible, in spite of the clotting traffic and the rain. Whenever she worked with Bernie, she felt as if he took more than half the load. It wasn't that he worked harder than she did; it was more that he was so calm and methodical that the days passed easily and efficiently.

Brierly Security sat incongruously above a loud and popular boutique like a bowler hat on a disco dancer. Anna ran up the poorly lit stairs with their white rubber treads, and was just in time to catch Beryl plugging in the night-line.

'I was just leaving,' Beryl said stiffly. 'Was it something?'

'Can I have a camera, please?' Anna asked, panting. She had run all the way from a nearby mews. Even so, she was parked on a double yellow line, and had to hurry.

'Well, you might have thought of that before you left this afternoon. I've locked up the requisition slips.'

'I'm sorry,' Anna said. One of the most maddening things about Beryl was that in matters of minutiæ she was generally right. 'I'm afraid I need the keys to the lock-up and one of the Commers too.' There was no point in asking Beryl to hurry. She had a knack of making Anna pay for any lapses, and keeping her waiting while she was parked illegally was just the sort of currency Beryl would use joyfully. As it was, she sorted through her keys with deliberate slowness and made Anna fill out three forms instead of one.

'It's just thoughtless,' Beryl complained. 'Why don't you learn to think ahead? You'd never catch Mr Schiller dashing in here at five to six, making me miss my train.'

This was perfectly true, but just then the truth was no comfort to Anna. She ran downstairs two at a time and sprinted to the car. Unfortunately, one of London's perverse traffic wardens had got there first. A contretemps with Beryl and a parking ticket could shatter Anna's sunniest mood. It was no way to end a working day, and she arrived home tired and irritable.

She let herself in at the front door, and found Selwyn Price blocking the way to her flat. He was sitting slumped halfway up the stairs looking like a reject from an Oxfam shop.

'I've got nowhere to go,' he said in a penetrating whisper directed at his own door on the ground floor. 'Bea's kicked me out again. She says I'm nine sheets to the wind and she wants my bloody carcass off her floor. She's hoovering. Women are so cruel when they're practical.'

Selwyn had had a drink or two, but he certainly wasn't drunk, although Anna knew that sometimes he pretended to be when he was extremely frustrated. It gave him the excuse he needed to misbehave. Bea, coming home from work, often hid from these outbursts behind her noisiest household tools.

'Well, get your bloody carcass off my stairs and come up,' Anna said. 'Your orphan on the doorstep role doesn't suit you at all.'

'Doesn't it?' Selwyn asked, jumping up and eagerly leading the way upstairs. 'I thought she might come out and see me here all lost and pathetic and be sorry, see?'

'Unlikely,' Anna said bluntly. 'Bea's got more sense than I have.'

'But this is better, isn't it? She won't be so keen to tip me out when she sees I've got somewhere to go.'

'Won't she?' Anna said, opening her own door. She thought Selwyn's tantrums were the product of an over-worked imagination and a sedentary life, and that Bea had more patience than he deserved. She was very fond of both of them but, she recognized ruefully, fonder of the sinner than the saint.

As she closed the door, she noticed Gene's raincoat hung neatly on a hanger in the tiny hall. Selwyn saw it too. 'I forgot,' he whispered, guiltily. 'It's the Yank: I let him in an hour ago.'

Anna was less enthusiastic about this news than she should have been. She had been hoping to have fried eggs on fried bread for supper. Now she would have to cook something more ambitious because Gene was not keen on fry-ups. She went into the living-room and Gene got up and kissed her.

It was one of Anna's best kept secrets that she did not like being kissed. It made her feel suffocated. She had never mentioned this to Gene so it wasn't his fault. But, as a new friend, she did blame him for greeting her intimately in front of an old one.

In fact, with unprecedented tact, Selwyn had dived into the kitchen, and could be heard rummaging in the fridge for a can of beer.

'Surprised?' Gene said, smiling brilliantly. Anna's bag slid off her shoulder on to the floor. He picked it up for her. 'I thought we could eat early and go out somewhere. How about it?'

'Well, we could eat early anyway,' she said awkwardly.

Selwyn came back dripping beer on to the carpet. 'I've put the kettle on,' he said. The two men eyed each other warily. Anna escaped to the kitchen and found that Selwyn had forgotten to light the gas.

'Have a glass of milk instead,' Gene called, 'you drink too much tea.' Anna turned on the gas anyway and reflected sadly that a man who really liked her would not be so quick to try and change her. Gene wanted a door key. Soon, she would have to stop shilly-shallying and come to some decision about it. Her milk bill had doubled in the months since she had known him. She examined the contents of the fridge. It would have to be a ham and mushroom omelette or an Indian takeaway, except that curries upset Gene's stomach.

Anna sighed. Her friendship with Gene was at that awkward stage where it might flower splendidly or equally it might turn into a bad habit. She could not make up her mind which was the more likely.

CHAPTER 2

It was a fresh clear morning, as if the clouds, having emptied themselves, had rolled away for a refill, leaving a temporary pale blue backdrop.

Anna left the Triumph in the street outside Mr Minh's garage where one of his several sons could find it. She jotted the licence number and her name on an envelope and posted the key through his letter-box. Mr Minh was an early riser, but it was only six-thirty and Anna couldn't hear a sound from behind the garage doors.

As she walked back past her old car she crossed her fingers for luck before stuffing her hands in her pockets and walking briskly south through Notting Hill Gate. It was half an hour's walk to the lock-up. Anna enjoyed it.

There were not many occasions when she could walk quickly through this part of London, crossing roads without much attention and breathing freely. Now the shops were shut and the hordes of consumers still tucked up in bed.

Anna manœuvred the Commer slowly out into the narrow alley. Too many people had driven it and the gearbox needed attention. It graunched and juddered from reverse to first, and she had to sail along in neutral for several yards before engaging the elusive second gear. At least, she thought, someone had attended to the chemical lavatory. She could not smell the combination of fecal and fungal that had made her last stint in the camper so unpleasant.

Bernie was waiting outside Belsize Park station. He heaved a well-filled carrier bag into the cab. Anna grinned.

'Loaves and fishes?' she asked. 'Sylvia's meals on wheels?'

'Leave it out,' Bernie said, smiling too. 'That's your breakfast and it's nearly pulled the arm off my shoulder.'

There was not an inch of parking space on either side of the street where Mrs Fourie lived. Anna swore and pulled up in front of someone's driveway.

'Not to worry,' Bernie said comfortably, 'one of these commuters'll let us in before this geezer wants to back out. Just keep on your toes.' He climbed into the back of the camper and began to unpack his bag. Anna divided her attention between the road and No. 29. Nothing happened. Bernie handed her the top of his Thermos flask filled with sweet white coffee.

It was eight o'clock before a likely space opened up.

'Hold tight,' Anna warned, and turned the key to start up. There was a click and an ominous silence.

'Oh balls, balls, and more balls,' she said venomously. She touched the horn. More silence.

'What's up?' Bernie asked.

'No electricity. Got a torch?' She tipped up the centre seat and Bernie shone a torch on the engine. She waggled some of the wiring with her left hand while twitching the key experimentally with her right. After a few seconds the engine turned over. She banged the camper into first gear and moved it into the vacant space.

'Dodgy,' commented Bernie. 'Is it something you can fix? We might have to push off in a hurry any time.'

'I think it's just a naff battery connection.'

'Well, see what you can do. I'll set up the bins.'

Anna disconnected the battery. There was a lot of corrosion on the terminals and connectors. She cleaned them and then fitted them together again. She turned the motor on and off several times, and each time it responded.

'Was it what you thought it was?' Bernie asked.

'I think so,' Anna said, looking for something to wipe her hands on. 'But if it goes kaput again, we'll know I'm wrong.' She had to settle for her own handkerchief in the end. 'If I *am* wrong, we'll be up a gum tree without a paddle because that's the only spanner in the tool kit and it's too big for any of the other connections.'

'Well, we'll have to cross that bridge when we come to it. Have some breakfast now and settle down.'

The binoculars were screwed to a small stand above the fire-extinguisher, and trained through a slight gap in the closed curtains. Bernie's Pentax, set up on a tripod, was likewise pointing its telephoto lens towards No. 29. Anna sat on the single bunk and busied herself with the packet of egg sandwiches Bernie gave her. When she had finished, she got the office Practika out of her bag, put in a roll of Tri-X and left the camera on the bunk beside her.

Bernie was listening to a talk about seal-culling on Radio Four and idly flipping through some photographs.

'Hey-up,' he said eventually. 'Action.'

Anna, looking through the binoculars, saw a couple emerge from the house.

'It's not her.' Bernie took a photograph anyway. 'Probably one of them from upstairs.'

It began to rain. Anna opened a window slightly to prevent the glass from steaming up.

Ten minutes later the door opened again, and two women appeared. One opened an umbrella and held it over the other while they came down the steps to the road. Their hair was of the sort that needed protection, Anna thought, as she watched them slide carefully into a red Mini and drive away.

'Top floor,' Bernie commented. 'One's a radiographer at Bart's and the other does something in the City. Or so Mr Fourie says.'

'What's he like?' Anna asked, sitting down and picking up the photographs. Some were of Janet Fourie, the others of her daughter, Claire.

'Sanctimonious old git.' Bernie uncorked his Thermos again and poured out the last of the coffee. 'Tell you what, though, first chance one of us gets, we should buy some tea-bags. This cupboard is bare except for a couple of tins of baked beans; Army surplus if you ask me.' He settled down again and continued, 'He lives in Hammersmith, nice place, quiet. But inside it's squared off like a soldier's bed. Everything at right angles and all bulled up. On top of that, he keeps washing his hands every ten minutes or so. Frankly, I'd be sorry if he did get custody of Claire. I wouldn't want to live with him if I was a fourteen-year-old girl.'

'Creepy?'

'Well, a bit. I must say, I kept asking myself if human life existed in that place. There were no paintings, for instance, just a lot of photographs of the Matterhorn or somewhere. All the books were either encyclopedias or

biographies. He has a hi-fi and some records, but they
were all Mozart, Bach, or Beethoven. Nothing else. I
went to the bathroom and it was chock-a-block with every
cleaning agent known to mankind; creams, powders, disinfectant, bleach, you name it. When I left, I thought he
couldn't wait to get on the blower to Rentokil and get the
place fumigated.'

'Well, no wonder Janet Fourie split.'

'Irretrievable breakdown, he said.'

'Whose?'

'Yes, well. To tell you the truth, I thought he was a bit
of a nutter. One of those obsessive blokes you'd hide the
chainsaw from.'

'As bad as that?'

'Could be. As a matter of fact, I think he even hears
voices.'

'Eerie!'

'Very funny,' Bernie said, 'but seriously, all of a
sudden, he'll cock his head on one side like a featherless
parrot and go all silent.'

'Blimey,' Anna said. 'Did you tell Mr Brierly?'

'Well, I did tip him the wink. But he thought it
sounded all right. They only spoke on the phone, you see.
All his nibs wanted to know was did I think Mr F would
have any trouble coughing up afterwards.'

'Typical. What about Claire? How does he get on with
her?'

'God knows,' Bernie said. 'He's got this picture of her
on his desk. She's all dressed in white for Confirmation.
Just like something out of *The Nun's Story*. But he's
getting worried. The school's not teaching her anything,
telly's rotting her brain, and now she's being corrupted by
her mother's boy-friends. In fact, everything's to blame
but human nature.'

'Well,' Anna said, looking at a photo of Claire, 'he's got
a tough row to hoe here. She looks more like something

off the front cover of *Penthouse* than a fourteen-year-old
schoolgirl.'

'Yes, she's a pretty kid,' Bernie said indifferently.
'Maybe it's something they put in the cod-liver oil these
days.'

'I wish they'd put some in mine, then.'

'Really?'

'No, not really,' Anna said thoughtfully. 'It can't be
easy being too pretty too young. So what do they do
together every Sunday?'

'You won't believe this, but he takes her to church.
Then, after lunch, he's got this woman who comes in and
gives her Latin lessons for an hour.'

'You're kidding!'

'It's true. Apparently, at school she had the choice
between taking Latin or German, and she chose German.
Well, he wasn't having that, but he couldn't get her to
change her mind. Hence the Sunday lessons.'

'What on earth does he think he's going to achieve by
that, except a very pissed-off daughter who knows some
Latin?'

'Search me. He's got a fixed idea about education that
doesn't take *her* into account at all.'

Rain pattered down on the metal roof like running
birds. The postman passed on his round. Car doors
slammed and engines revved, but no one else emerged
from No. 29.

Bernie had a talent for waiting. It came from long
practice. He could relax completely and remain alert at
the same time. Anna wished she could do it too, but when
she relaxed she was in danger of nodding off and it was
difficult to keep her attention on the door they were
watching without getting fidgety. Later, the milkman
called, but even the clunking bottles drew no response.
Two pints stood dripping on the doorstep until nearly

half past ten. Then the door opened and an arm reached out.

Bernie and Anna listened to *Story Time* and the news. Then Bernie put a tape in the cassette recorder and they listened to that.

At last Mrs Fourie appeared carrying a laundry bag. She walked towards Haverstock Hill. Anna went too, more for the fresh air than anything else. Mrs Fourie wasn't dressed for anything but a trip to the launderette. Anna bought tea-bags and toilet-paper and then found a phone-box. First she checked in at the office. Nothing was happening there either, except that Beryl had hay-fever. After that, Anna crossed her fingers and called Mr Minh.

'Sorry, sorry, Miss Lee,' Mr Minh said, in his high rapid voice, 'no MOT. Chassis members, cross-members all finish. I tell you last year she not live another winter.'

'But surely, if I did a bit more welding,' Anna said without much hope.

'Sorry, sorry, no more welding. All weld and no chassis already.'

'But the engine and the tyres are still good.'

'Yes, yes, engine clean as new whistle. Lovely job,' Mr Minh said soothingly. 'But your body letting you down.'

Anna giggled. Mr Minh, who hated to give bad news, thought she was taking it rather well. 'Tell you what,' he said cheerfully, 'I know a man got a Triumph Herald. Good body, cracked cylinder head, lots of things finish in engine.'

'You think we could swap engines?' Anna asked.

'Swap, yes. Very cheap.'

'Give me a price.' Mr Minh always knew a man, and he could always give a price in five seconds flat.

'That's steep!' Anna protested when she heard it.

'Throw in MOT,' said Mr Minh, who had never come to terms with fixed prices.

'All the same . . .'

'Tell you what, I know a man with Renault Four you can drive this week, OK?'

'OK,' Anna said. 'It's a deal.'

'Good deal. I'm sorry she clap out proper this time.'

The afternoon passed in stuffy tedium. This did not distress Anna as much as it might have had she not had a sneaking belief that wages *should* be earned in hours of boredom. Any largesse that ever came her way by other means, the insurance money of a few months ago, a small bequest from a great-uncle, was unearned and a little immoral. To work was to be bored and it sometimes gave her satisfaction to be so bored and thus so worthy of her hire.

'There's more than a narrow streak of the puritan in you,' Selwyn protested, when he heard this unlikely commentary. 'I'm telling you, girl, there's no virtue in any mortification, either of the flesh or the spirit. So get down off your high horse and have a little rhubarb crumble.'

'It seems such a waste of money, though,' Bea said, pouring a generous yellow dollop of custard on three plates. Her judgments were neither moral nor poetic. 'I mean, it's two of you he's paying for, isn't it? And by the hour, too. What on earth can this man expect that will justify such an expense?'

'Search me,' Anna said. 'Usually, they want to get back at their ex-wives for some reason, and the child hardly comes into it at all. But in this case, our esteemed client seems such an odd bloke that I wouldn't want to speculate what his reasons might be.'

'So why do it?' Selwyn loved unanswerable questions. 'It sounds to me as if the virtuous father would be a far less suitable parent than the mother. Whatever her failings, at least she seems human.'

'Well, I can't pick and choose who I work for, can I?

And besides, if there is any evidence, he has to take it to his solicitor who decides whether it's worth anything. And after that, a court decides whether or not to act on it. Nine times out of ten there's no evidence and nothing happens.'

They ate in silence for a few minutes. Bea made real custard with eggs. 'Just occasionally,' Anna went on, licking her spoon regretfully, 'you do come across some kid who's being mistreated or abused and that makes it all worthwhile.'

'If something's done about it,' Bea stipulated, collecting the dishes for seconds. 'But still, it's an awful waste of money.'

'My living isn't a waste of money,' Anna protested. But Bea did not look convinced.

CHAPTER 3

Really, there was no way that Anna could properly claim that watching a front door for seven hours at a stretch was anything but a waste of time and money. But in order to fulfil her obligation to the firm and to the client who paid the firm, this was what she had to do. If she had been on her own, she would have come to loathe the blank blue surface very quickly. As it was, with Bernie's company, the hours could be relieved by all sorts of small actions: making tea, scanning the paper, trying to mend Bernie's alarm clock.

In the afternoon, when they had just learned that rain had stopped play again at Lord's, and the pitch had been covered, Janet Fourie emerged wheeling a plastic shopping-basket. Anna dutifully followed her round the local shops and returned to find Bernie grinning with quiet amusement.

'Little devil,' he said, 'she only waits till her mum's round the corner, and then she nips off down the hill for a packet of Number Six and half a bottle of vodka. We ought to be on our toes now. I bet you the cat's going out this evening and the mouse is getting ready to play.'

They decided that Bernie should follow Janet Fourie, while Anna would take Claire. 'I might get arrested, running round behind her after dark,' Bernie said, 'and anyway, if there's any running to do your legs are younger than mine. Plodding I can just about manage. But the younger generation doesn't plod, so it's all yours.'

If Mrs Fourie left by car or taxi, it seemed best that Bernie should take Anna's borrowed Renault. They reasoned that Claire would not have bought drink and cigarettes unless her mother were going out, and then it was most likely that she would stay at home and invite friends in.

'It's about time,' Anna grumbled. 'They don't exactly have a scorching social life, do they?'

'Well, we've only been here two days,' Bernie protested. 'Actually, Mum teaches remedials at the same Comprehensive Claire goes to, so I expect she's knackered come the end of term.'

In fact, when Janet Fourie appeared, just before six, she looked nothing like a tired schoolteacher. In startling contrast to the sensible but unglamorous woman who had gone shopping earlier in the afternoon, this Mrs Fourie was slim and elegant in a cream linen suit. With her hair done up in a loose knot on top of her head, and high-heeled shoes, she looked younger and taller and there was a spring in her step and a sparkle in her eye that had been missing previously.

'Sure you don't want to change your mind?' Anna asked. 'Mum doesn't look much like a plodder tonight.'

'Give me the strength,' Bernie sighed, rolling his eyes up as he disappeared from the back of the camper. Mrs

Fourie got into the cab that had come to collect her and drove off towards Haverstock Hill with Bernie trundling sedately behind.

It was a refreshing evening. The trees shone from a recent shower, but the sky was a clear fading blue. It seemed as if a momentary lull had overtaken London's noise. Or perhaps it was because Anna was now alone and the only sounds she heard were those she made herself. The effect was soporific, so that when Claire Fourie came out, Anna nearly missed her. One minute, she was idly watching the couple from upstairs come home, and the next, Claire was running down the stone steps. They must have passed in the hall. Luckily, no one had come to pick her up, and she walked purposefully off in the opposite direction from the one her mother had taken.

Anna pulled herself together and followed. It was a brisk walk, but she had time to admire Claire's back as they went along. Her blonde wavy hair was parted low at one side and caught back with a single comb behind her ear on the other. It swayed across her shoulders, dancing with light and vitality. The hair was young, but the style was mature, and there was no hint of immaturity in the body. Claire, though small, was in perfect proportion without a trace of either coltishness or puppy-fat. The major deceit, however, was in her movements. She walked like a woman and not like a schoolgirl who played netball and rounders. Anna could now easily forgive the person in the off-licence who had sold Claire drink and cigarettes. From the way she dressed, it was obvious that Claire wanted to encourage any mistakes other people made about her age.

Anna wondered why. As a teenager she had been a skinny kid who hadn't fooled anyone much. There had been times when she had wanted to: trying to get into cinemas to see X-rated films, for instance. But the efforts had only been occasional. Mainly, she had felt a sort of pride about not being grown-up. She had not admired the adults she knew and so she had not been eager to imitate them.

Claire, it seemed, was the opposite. It looked as if consistent practice had gone into that walk and the air of ennui with which she ignored the people who looked at her. And a lot of people did look at her. Anna could not see her face, of course, but she felt sure that Claire was quite conscious of the effect she was making. Just following her, Anna became self-conscious too, as if she were a minor character in procession behind the principal girl: not worthy of much attention, but part of the show all the same.

They reached the lower limits of Hampstead Heath and Claire turned off the road. The brisk pace dropped. She was no longer hurrying, but strolling as if she had all the time in the world. In this way, they came to the Ponds, where Claire joined two other girls and a young man who were obviously waiting for her. One of the girls was annoyed and looked at her watch as she approached.

Anna walked steadily past them and stopped a few yards further on to look at the water. But the group soon started off, overtaking her. As they passed, she heard Claire say casually, 'Yeah, but there were things to do,' in reply to some complaint from the girl who was annoyed. She let them get a fair distance ahead and then turned in pursuit. They walked round the Ponds and turned right on to the foot of Parliament Hill.

There were plenty of people about: walking, jogging, or exercising their dogs. The light was fading slowly, and the grass had begun to take on its evening luminance, but it was still far from dusk. Two men got up out of the grass, and the four ahead of Anna waved and went over. Anna altered her direction and walked on until some trees came between them. Then she doubled back. She was not close enough to hear anything that was said or even to see features clearly, so she got the Practika out of her bag and focussed the telephoto lens on them. They were sitting down in a rough circle now. Claire's bottle of vodka was being passed around, and they seemed to be talking and laughing. Anna could not tell who was with whom. She clicked off a couple of frames while it was still light enough and then, opening the aperture fully, continued to watch them through the lens.

She had the light behind her, and a tree-trunk to blend into. All the same, she was clearly visible if anyone cared to look. Nobody did, they were too engrossed in their own activities. She watched one of the men licking cigarette papers and sticking them together. The others looked on. It was a dreary ritual. Anna put the camera down and sat leaning against the tree. The air was still. You could light a match without protecting the flame. The joint-maker did, and after a few deep pulls, passed it on and lay back in the grass looking exhausted.

Anna wasn't very good at estimating people's ages, but none of the six looked much older than twenty. Even so, Claire must have been the youngest by three or four years. Anna wondered if the others knew it. For a girl of fourteen, Claire had displayed a fair collection of bad habits in the last few minutes: booze, smoke, and now dope. Was she doing it because these were her true appetites, or was it part of the act? Either way, she was taking a risk and it was a depressing sight. There was nothing very harmful in it really, but Anna stared up at the dark turquoise sky and felt uneasy for her.

Unaware of her silent scrutiny, the friends happily shared the joint and bottle. She could hear their laughter but not the jokes. Perhaps they didn't need the jokes. She watched a golden retriever running in large circles around them with its nose down, looking for something. Not finding whatever it was, the dog stood facing her, sniffing the air. Finally, he made up his mind and bounded over to her, waving his yellow plumed tail and greeting her like an old friend.

'Wrong again,' Anna said, stroking the handsome head, 'sorry, pal, but you'll have to try a little harder.' She picked up a stick and threw it behind her, hoping to encourage the dog to search for the scent again. But, although he ran off, he soon returned and joyfully dropped the wet trophy on her lap. Then he lay down close to her. 'Any port in a storm, eh?' Anna said. 'Well, it's a hard lesson to learn, but anything is not necessarily better than nothing.' She threw the stick again, but this time the dog didn't stir. She looked for a name tag, but he had none, and she got her hands licked wet for her trouble.

'An old softy with no name,' she said, giving him a gentle push. 'Go on, shove off now. I've got work to do and I don't want a dog with no moral fibre.' The dog laid its head on her knee and gazed at her with unreserved love.

'I don't believe a word of it,' she said, quite crossly. If she had anything against dogs, it was that they dumped adoration and dependence on humans for no reason whatsoever. But she gave up trying to get rid of him in case it made her conspicuous.

As darkness came, the six people on the grass got up and walked down towards the path. They were hard to see, but Anna didn't bother much until they seemed to melt into the wall of the gardens that backed on to the hill. Then she began to run. The dog ran with her, barking excitedly and jumping up every now and then to nip her sleeve. Shaking him off, she raced to the wall and found that some of the houses had doors from their gardens that led directly on to the Heath. The wall was a high one and she couldn't see over it. Claire was gone.

Anna sprinted along the wall and came to an alley which linked the Heath with the road. She ran along it and found herself on a street of large houses. She tried to work out which house Claire had gone into, but there were more houses than there had been gates, and after a while she gave up. What was worse: there was nowhere she could wait unobserved until Claire came out again.

'Oh, shoot and stuff it,' she hissed, and trudged down to South End Green. The dog, still attached as if by an invisible leash, now walked quietly at her side. 'If you're so bloody well-trained,' she said sourly, 'how come you got lost in the first place?'

There was nothing to do but wait. Anna went into a café and ordered a poached egg on toast. If Claire came home on foot she would have to pass the café. If she were driven, Anna wouldn't see her anyway. It didn't make any difference now, but at least she wanted to avoid the shame of arriving back at the camper alone.

'No dogs!' said the girl who brought her egg. 'I'm afraid you'll have to tie him up outside.'

There wasn't much point in denying ownership of a dog that had so obviously adopted her, so Anna took him out. 'Just don't get run over now,' she said, thinking that all she needed was to worry about an animal that wasn't hers in the first place. He sat guarding the door.

It was nearly ten o'clock before Claire passed by. She was with one of the men from the Heath and he had a black leather arm draped casually over her shoulders. As they turned the corner Anna caught a glimpse of a sharp profile under short hair like seal-skin. She left the café, and a wet nose searching for her hand told her that her four-legged friend still hadn't given up.

At the end of Claire's street, the couple split up, exchanging a few intense words, and a little further on, Claire stopped. She scrubbed at her face with a tissue and dropped it into the gutter. Taking the comb out of her hair, she parted it in the middle and fastened each side into bunches. Then she walked steadily back home and

let herself in through the front door. Anna saw lights go
on in the Fouries' flat. She glanced round the empty street
and then unlocked the camper.

Ten minutes later, while she was writing an
abbreviated report in her notebook she glanced up and
saw the boy who had been with Claire arrive in front of
the house. He went down the steps and the lights went on
in the basement flat.

'Well, there's a turn-up,' she muttered. In the two days
she and Bernie had spent watching the house, neither of
them had noticed any sign of life from the basement. She
wondered whether to risk sneaking into the front garden
and taking a look through the window. But a couple of
seconds later curtains were drawn across the barred
windows.

Mrs Fourie came home less than an hour later, and
Bernie appeared a few minutes after her. 'What's this
then? The Tail-Waggers Club?' he asked as he climbed
into the back, and fended off the retriever's enthusiastic
welcome.

'Don't start,' Anna said wearily. 'God knows I've tried
to get rid of him. And he's eaten your roll-mops. I
couldn't stop him.'

'Well, you can take him to the police later,' he said,
patting the dog, who seemed to think Bernie a softer
touch than Anna. 'In the meantime, we'd better swap
stories. I talked to the office earlier and tomorrow Phil
and Johnny are replacing us here, because I'm serving an
injunction, and you're reporting to the customer.'

'Already?' Anna said. 'But we've hardly got stuck in yet.'

'He's keen as mustard, apparently,' Bernie said. 'Wants
to see if we're on our toes. The old keen-eyed sleuth lark.'

'Well, dead-eyed dick is all he's getting from me,
mate,' Anna said. 'Actually, it looks as though Mr
Fourie's little Claire is playing right into his hands. She
could do with a bit of restraint, like a ball and chain.'

CHAPTER 4

'As a matter of fact, I agree with you,' Mr Brierly said unexpectedly. It was a rare occurrence and Anna stared at him in some surprise. 'Unless we tone your findings down a little, Mr Fourie might jump to premature conclusions.'

Anna was seated across the desk from Mr Brierly on one of his bruising office chairs. It was the sort of chair only comfortable to those who are well-cushioned themselves. Mr Brierly liked to keep interviews short.

He, on the other hand, had assumed his favourite position, tipped back comfortably on his orthopaedic swivel chair with his fingers laced over his waistcoat, thumbs revolving steadily. He swung round so that he could look out over Kensington High Street.

'What should I do then?' Anna asked. 'Strain the lumps out?'

'In a manner of speaking,' Mr Brierly said to the double-glazing. 'After all, you can't be one hundred per cent positive it was marijuana in those cigarettes.'

'Well, there's no reason to make a three-paper joint out of perfectly good cigarettes unless you put something in it,' she suggested tentatively.

'Of course, you'd know more about that than I would,' he said nastily. 'But I suggest we leave that part till later, when there's some firmer proof.' He looked at his gold Timex. 'And now, since I am expecting Mr Fourie in forty-five minutes' time, I further suggest that you combine your notes with Mr Schiller's in a legible way, and have them ready when he arrives.'

Mr Brierly's suggestions were Anna's orders, so she installed herself in the Report Room with a strong cup of

Maxwell House for company. It was a tiny room with no
windows and most of the floor space was taken up by two
steel desks placed at right angles to each other with chairs
on both sides. This was supposed to be accommodation
for four, but in practice, if even two people had to work
together there, they had to leave the door into the
corridor open for air. Anyone else needing to write a
report at the same time would take a typewriter into the
rec-room. Such space as there was was further limited by
green filing cabinets and piles of large books such as
Archbold's *Criminal Evidence and Pleading*, Stone's
Justices' Manual, and an over-generous supply of dusty
telephone directories.

Anna left the door open as a matter of habit. She did
not like confined places, and five minutes in the Report
Room produced a choking sensation only equalled by the
tube at rush-hour.

Given the choice, she would probably admit to a
preference for typing up a report over serving an
injunction, but the choice never seemed to come her way.
Nowadays she didn't even bother to comment. That was
the way the cards were dealt, and while Beryl was firmly
in charge of the whole pack it would never be any other
way.

'A woman's place is on her arse,' she muttered,
squinting at her notes. She had to admit, too, that she
had less trouble with Bernie's writing than she did with
her own, which looked as if a drunken spider with ink on
its feet had run around and died on the paper, whereas
Bernie's was so neat it might have been already typed. She
took a deep breath and started to type her usual sonata
for two fingers.

When Beryl called her through to the main office, Mr
Fourie had already arrived. He was standing with his
hands behind his back in the centre of the room, a tall,
emaciated man wearing a pale grey suit that matched his

pale grey hair.

'You have already met Mr Schiller,' Mr Brierly said. 'This is Miss Lee who is also engaged in your affair.'

Mr Fourie nodded but made no move to shake hands. Mr Brierly seemed a little at a loss. It was obvious that Mr Fourie had not yet sat down, and equally obvious that he was not going to. Anna knew that Mr Brierly's rigid code of manners required that the client took a seat before he settled himself behind the desk. Anna smiled. She handed copies of her report to the two men. Mr Fourie began to read his immediately while Mr Brierly shifted his weight uncomfortably. They stood there like three storks in a pond. Finally Anna took the initiative and sat down, which released Mr Brierly to do the same.

She examined Mr Fourie with interest. Bernie was right, there was indeed something of the demented parrot about him, the head on one side, little shuffling bobbing movements and a fastidious unblinking gaze over his short beaky nose. It was hard to believe that he was Claire's father or that he had ever been married to Janet Fourie. Perhaps he couldn't believe it either. He held Anna's report in the tips of his fingers, as far away as he reasonably could, as if it were some obscene weapon which might explode in his face.

By mistake, she caught Mr Brierly's eye. He looked away quickly but avoided fixing his gaze on Mr Fourie. He had become noticeably anxious. It was beginning to dawn on him that his client was something more than a worried parent.

Perversely, Anna began to feel almost sorry for Mr Fourie. A man of his appearance could only be a figure of fun. But such a man was probably very sick or unhappy or both. Unfortunately, he would probably be a disaster as a father too. Sympathy had to stop somewhere.

When Mr Fourie had finished reading, he put the papers on the desk, saying, 'I would like to wash my hands,' and Beryl was summoned to show him to the cloakroom.

There was a silence while he was out of the room. Mr Brierly would not allow himself to comment, but his eyebrows were rather nearer to his hairline than usual. Anna wondered what Mr Fourie would make of Brierly Security's washbasins, and when he came back she noticed that his hands were still wet. Anna was not surprised. The roller-towel was sometimes dirty enough to defeat the object of washing in the first place.

'Well, now,' he said in a precise tenor voice, 'this person my wife was out with last night, what can you tell me about him?'

After a nod from Brierly, Anna said, 'Nothing yet, Mr Fourie. As you can see, he lives in a respectable part of town, and Mr Schiller didn't see anything out of the ordinary about his behaviour.'

'What you have failed to grasp, Miss Lee,' he replied, in a clipped punctilious tone, 'is that, while my wife was fornicating with this person, she was neglecting my daughter.'

Even Mr Brierly seemed rather stunned by this so Anna said, 'As far as Mr Schiller was aware, there was no misconduct. In fact, he points out that their behaviour was quite formal. Besides,' she added lamely, 'they went to the pictures.'

'My wife,' Mr Fourie went on, as if he hadn't heard a word, 'has always been lax in her morals, lax in her behaviour, in her standards, and in matters of hygiene. This was not too apparent while she was under my control and influence. But she has always neglected my daughter and now the results are plainly disastrous.'

Anna could think of nothing else to say to him. The man was clearly a loony and she wondered how Mr Brierly would deal with him. She remembered with relief that she had taken the hint and left the marijuana out of her report, but she wished now that she had left some other things out too.

Mr Fourie coughed, a tiny hiccupping sound, and resumed: 'Of course, I could bring an action against the person who sold alcohol and nicotine to my daughter, but that is begging the question. That my daughter is willing to introduce such poisons into her system is because of my wife's appalling influence. No such thing would have occurred had she been in my care.'

'I have always found it unwise to underestimate the influence of a child's peer group,' Mr Brierly intervened at last. 'Teenagers are notoriously difficult to supervise. I realize that this is very distressing for you,' he went on, although Mr Fourie showed no sign of distress at all, 'but we have not yet established that your wife's conduct has been anything but exemplary.'

'The atmosphere of the home is of prime importance,' Mr Fourie said reasonably, 'and can either benefit or contaminate a child. Every child needs careful guidance and my daughter is no exception if she is not to be soiled by the values of the world today.'

'Quite so,' Mr Brierly said, hurriedly getting to his feet. He was obviously eager to end the meeting before it got out of hand. At the very least his clients should demonstrate a minimum degree of sanity; unfortunately, Mr Fourie fell somewhat short of this minimum. 'It has been most instructive to meet you. Shall we leave it that we will be in touch the minute we have any more news to interest you?' He switched on the intercom. 'Miss Doyle? Miss Doyle will attend to the details.'

'It is a mystery to me why my wife was given custody of my daughter. You would think the courts would know better.' Mr Fourie fixed his pale grey eyes on Anna for the first time. 'But then, a certain type of woman can be most persuasive.' His skin was as pale and dry as paper. 'That is why I need unbiased and objective proof that my wife is the source of corruption.'

Some reply seemed to be expected, but Anna was saved by Beryl who came in and stood by the door. She and Mr Brierly exchanged a long expressionless look. He said, 'Well, Mr Fourie, it was good of you to come. If you will accompany Miss Doyle, she will take care of everything.'

'A cheque will be fine for now,' Beryl said, purposefully circling Mr Fourie and manœuvring him through the door.

Anna knew that Mr Brierly was embarrassed although he showed no sign of it. A private agency has more than its fair share of requests from unbalanced people, but normally he was very astute at weeding out those who would give his business a bad name. Whatever the outcome of a case, he did his best to ensure that his reputation did not suffer, and that his firm was seen to act in a respectable and judicious way.

Mr Brierly liked to think of himself as a man of sound judgement and he did not like his mistakes to be witnessed. That the witness of this error should be the youngest and least respected of his employees was something Anna hoped she would not have to suffer for.

'He's gone now,' Beryl said over the intercom, 'and the account is paid up for a full week.'

Mr Brierly looked relieved. 'Well, Miss Lee, we shall have to proceed with caution. I hope I can rely on your discretion.' He should not have said that, but Anna, who had been expecting something much worse, nodded seriously and went while the going was good. She had the rest of the day off.

CHAPTER 5

There was a long queue outside the Royal Academy. It was a dark grey afternoon, meanly spitting rain.

'Jeeze, I'm not waiting in this,' Gene said, eyeing the slowly moving mass of disconsolate art-lovers.

'Not even for Monet?' Anna asked mischievously. They had come on a pilgrimage to see Gene's favourite painting.

'Not even for money,' he replied smartly and Anna made a sign with her finger that awarded him a point.

'Wait here,' he said, and ran to the head of the queue, the skirt of his fawn raincoat billowing like a jaunty sail. He disappeared into the crowd. Anna pulled up the collar of her coat and dug her hands deep in her pockets. After a while he came back, accompanied by an Academy porter who was carrying a huge black umbrella.

'This way, your ladyship,' the porter said in a whisper that could be heard all around the forecourt. He held the umbrella over Anna's head and hurried her towards the entrance. She directed a horrified glare at Gene as people in the queue turned to stare and mutter crossly among themselves.

'Thenk you,' Anna said distantly as the porter ushered them in past the waiting crowd and the security bench. 'So kind.'

'It's an honour,' he said simply, directing them up the stairs.

'What on earth did you tell him?' Anna asked when they were out of earshot. But Gene just laid a finger on his lips and looked mysterious.

'Some people will do anything for Monet,' she hissed. 'You want to watch out, Monet corrupts.'

He smiled his snowy smile but refused to award her a point. They raced round the exhibition until Gene found the picture he was looking for. He stopped and inspected it from all angles, stepping close to examine the brush work. After five minutes he stood back.

'The postcard was better,' he said in tones of deepest disappointment. Anna sat down on a bench, weak from suppressed laughter.

'I'm serious,' he said glumly. 'I've carried this goddamned postcard around with me for eight years. A girl sent it to me from Paris. She said it was the most beautiful painting in the whole world.'

'Well, it *is* lovely,' she said, still laughing.

'Yeah, but the earth didn't move,' he said flatly.

'Oh, if that's all you want, why didn't you say so? We could've saved ourselves the bother and got a hot-fudge sundae instead. You can't eat art.'

'Now you're talking!' Gene's eyes lit up. 'Come on.' He set off towards the exit. Anna got up and followed. She could see his crisp fair hair as people surged between them, and he weaved his way swiftly through the gallery. His enthusiasm was irresistible; it was as if he had never been disappointed in his life. He approached everything without fear of failure. Anna smiled. It was a pity they couldn't spend their lives simply gadding.

They walked arm in arm down Piccadilly to the Hard Rock Café where he charmed the waitress into showing them to a quiet table. Women responded to his exuberance, Anna noticed, whereas men saw it as aggression and treated him with caution.

The ice-cream came, covered in steaming rich sauce and dotted with nuts. 'You know what?' Gene said, eagerly digging his spoon into the sweet mound. 'We'll go sailing this weekend. How about that? I know a guy with a cottage and a boat down in Weymouth.'

Only a few months ago she had been his only contact in

London; now he had more invitations and friends than she did. He had scraped together every acquaintance open to him, and from the crowd had found a surprising number of good friends. Perhaps it was easier for a foreigner. There was less competition or mistrust, and above all no threat of permanence.

'There's going to be a party down there,' he went on, spooning up the last of the sundae, 'and we're going to sail over to the Isle of Wight.'

'Sorry,' Anna said regretfully, 'I can't. I'm working this weekend.'

'Oh no. I thought you said the case you were on was a dead end.'

'It is. But after all, the bloke's paid for a full week. We can't just dump it like a dead frog and fake the reports.'

'I don't see why not. You're not going to tell the guy anything anyway. It's a waste of time. Why don't you just plead sick or something?'

'Because I don't fancy being on the dole.'

'Come on! There must be some way around it. Why are you letting it screw up your life?'

'People with jobs these days,' Anna said, in what she hoped was a tone of finality, 'don't bugger them up for a pleasant weekend. Replacements are hard to come by.'

'Crap!' Gene said. What had started lightly enough was becoming more serious. 'It wouldn't come to that.'

'Wouldn't it? Everybody's cutting back. One dodgy move from me could provide Mr B with his first economy. Look, Gene,' she said, trying to relieve the tension, 'it's stopped raining now, let's forget it and go to the pictures or something.'

'No,' he said tersely. 'Let's talk about it. You know this isn't the first time. Having a job is one thing, but working unreasonable hours week after week is something else. It seems to me that you get all the late hours and weekends they fork out, and you don't stand up for yourself.'

'Well, most of the others have wives and families, but they do work weekends when they have to.'

'When they have to? Well, what about me? You're never around when I'm free. Look, I'm not possessive, but either you're my woman or you're not.'

A couple of seconds passed and then they burst out laughing. It was too ridiculous.

'That's what I like about him,' Anna said later, when she was having a final cup of tea with Selwyn and Bea before going upstairs to bed. 'He says these awful things, but they're just as silly to him as they are to me.'

'He has got wonderful teeth. That much I will admit,' Selwyn said absently. The Prices were playing Scrabble, a dangerous occupation for such a marriage. Bea played with Chambers at her elbow and bravely thwarted most of Selwyn's attempts to enrich the English language.

'You ought to be more careful though,' Bea said, laying TROUSER meticulously on the board. 'Chaps don't wait forever.'

'Chap or job,' Anna grumbled. 'Maybe you're right. One of these days he won't laugh and I'll be out of a chap again.'

'That's what I mean,' Bea said, nodding earnestly without taking her eyes off the board. 'Selwyn, there's no such word as UNTROUSERED. You have to give in now and then, Anna.'

'Well, you aren't setting much of an example,' Selwyn snapped, substituting RUNE with bad grace. 'You're sounding very bloodless, Leo. It's not as if the poor man is trying to put you out of work, he just wants to see more of you.' Bea laid out NOTE.

'I know, I know,' Anna said sadly. 'But I've seen the danger signs before, and it makes me nervous. He's a smashing man and I love going out with him but there's something wrong when we're at home. Oh well, I expect

I'm just feeling rushed.' Selwyn spelled out OZAENA and leaned back with a satisfied smirk.

'What's that?' Bea said disbelievingly.

'Look it up, woman,' he said, triumphantly. 'It's one of the most disgusting words in the dictionary, and it's taken care of my Z.'

CHAPTER 6

'Who's the joker at the bottom of the woodpile?' Johnny asked. It was Saturday morning, and Anna was sharing the watch with Johnny Crocker. Bernie would relieve him on Sunday.

'The boy-friend in the basement?' Anna said, chewing on a digestive biscuit for breakfast. Standards definitely dropped when Bernie was away. 'I don't know who he is. The lease is held by a Greta Hall. I checked with the landlord yesterday.'

'Well, it ain't her.' Johnny brushed sausage-roll crumbs from his moustache, the one remaining feature of his military background. Otherwise, he affected a sloppy flamboyance, and grew his curly black hair rather longer than Mr Brierly might have wished. 'Four of them went in there last night. It looks like Rowton House to me.'

'What about Claire? Did she go down there?'

'Not on your life. Cute little Claire wouldn't do anything that straightforward. She's a talented little intriguer, isn't she? You should've seen her yesterday,' he said admiringly. 'She comes out of here like Harriet, Heroine of St Hilda's, with a pile of books, and trips along to the library. Butter wouldn't melt. Then a quick change to Babydoll behind Biographies and she's off down the Labour Exchange to meet Jumpin' Jack Flash.'

'The Labour Exchange?' Anna laughed. 'How very idyllic.'

'Yeah, romance can't bloom too sweet in that sort of place. Still, a man's got to do what a man's got to do, even if it's only signing on. There but for the grace of whoever go the rest of us.'

'Quite,' Anna said superstitiously. 'Are the other four still in there?'

'I didn't see anyone come out. Truth is, I didn't see them too well going in. I never thought to bring the nightscope.' He yawned. 'Not that it matters. Christ, I'm so bloody bored. What do you say to a quick shufty round the back? Just to liven the show up a bit. My bum's getting paralysed.'

'Hardly wise or politic,' Anna said in a fair imitation of Mr Brierly.

'Oh, stuff wise and politic! There's no one around. I'll toss you for it.' He flipped a penny and called tails. But when they eventually found the coin among the rubbish on the floor, it was heads. 'Lucky old you.'

'Oh, very lucky,' Anna said resignedly. 'What's a little bit of trespass between friends?'

'I won't tell anyone,' Johnny said, pushing her towards the door.

'Oh well, of what you are about to perceive may the Lord make you truly forgetful. Bail me out if I'm caught.'

'If you're caught, I never met you,' he said cheerfully.

Anna crossed the road quickly, making sure no one was watching from either No. 29 or its immediate neighbours, and went down the side steps to the basement. The kitchen window was barred like the front one. Looking through it, her first impression was that it was lavishly endowed with nothing but empty milk bottles. A second look confirmed this and she went on past the door to the garden gate. The back garden had a shaggy unkempt look to it. It did not seem entirely neglected, because the lawn was well mown, but more as if someone liked it that way. Iron steps led up to a door into the first-floor flat, so it was probably the Fouries' garden. It was separated from the basement area by a thin hedge of buddleia bushes and a single wire stretching between the neighbour's fence and the gate. Anna stepped over the wire and between the bushes. The gate looked more likely to fall over than to open quietly. Two basement windows faced the garden. One was barred and the other was a pair of French windows.

She looked first through the barred window into a dark and dirty bathroom. It was hard to believe that the bath had ever been white. Grey rings had merged together to give the appearance of stratified slate. A couple of dingy towels were slung carelessly over the edge. The lavatory had no seat, and the washbasin was cracked. She moved on to the French windows. The curtains there were falling off their rails, and looking through the gap she thought at first that everyone inside was dead. Two fully clothed bodies were sprawled across uncovered mattresses as if they had been dropped from a great height, and two sleeping-bags like overstuffed bolsters lay beside them. She stepped back and looked up at the Fouries' back windows. They were slightly open and fresh coloured curtains stirred quietly in the morning breeze. Anna went back to the camper.

'You're right,' she told Johnny, 'it's just like a doss house, a proper mess.'

'Funny, isn't it, when everyone upstairs seems so respectable,' he said thoughtfully. 'You'd think someone would've complained to the landlord. It makes you wonder what's in it for bourgeois little Claire.'

'Excitement?' Anna reached for the Thermos flask. 'The fun of having one over on the grown-ups? Kids are one of life's mysteries, aren't they? Everyone's been one but nobody understands them.'

'You can say that again with flaming knobs on,' Johnny said. 'Look, can you hold the fort for a few minutes? I

want to go down the road for some milk and a quick call
to my bookie.'

Nothing out of the ordinary happened until early
afternoon when a young girl wearing jeans and a T-shirt
arrived on the doorstep. She was let in and a few minutes
later came out again with Claire.

'Swimming?' Johnny said, pointing out the rolled towel
in Claire's straw bag. 'This one's yours. Not that I'd mind
doing a stint in the ladies' changing-room.'

Anna followed the two girls to the Swiss Cottage Baths.
Claire's companion was a big girl and judging by the
shortness of her trousers, still growing. She looked
awkward and gawky next to Claire, and Anna felt sorry
for her. She was several inches taller, but looked a lot
younger. The impression was strengthened by the way she
seemed to devour Claire's conversation, looking at her
constantly, while Claire hardly looked her way at all. In
fact, the angle of Claire's head and the tilt of her
shoulders spoke of complete boredom.

It was a good day for swimming. A lot of people
thought so, a constant stream of them wandered in and
out of the sports centre looking sleepy and bemused.
Everyone seemed dazed by the sudden good weather. The
market was busy too: traders and customers smiling at the
sun. And it seemed to be a day out for the local ashram.
The faithful, in gaudy orange, each with a necklace of
cedar beads, blew like confetti through the stolid crowd.
Londoners took off their jackets and cardigans and rolled
up their sleeves perhaps for the first time that year. By
contrast, the three winos, sharing a stone bench and a
bottle, were as wrapped and wadded as they had been in
midwinter.

Anna could have waited in the shade of the foyer once
she had made sure that the girls were really going to the
pool. But she chose to stay outside in the sun. It was both

a good and a poor place to wait. Good, because in the
toing and froing from the pool and the market anyone
could hang around and not be noticed; poor, because the
best view of the pool entrance, the walkway, and the road
was from a makeshift car park which was dirty and
uncomfortable. Anna sat back against the sloping bonnet
of a Citroën and hoped that the owner was in no hurry.

She longed for a can of cold lager but decided not to
risk going off to find one. Since her failure on the Heath
when she had lost Claire, she was determined to brush up
her street-work and not allow her concentration to lapse.
So in the next hour or so she became quite fond of the
Citroën. It made a perfect shooting-stick. The sloping
bonnet seemed to have been designed to accommodate
any length of leg. She would have been far from comfortable if there had been only Minis and Cortinas to choose
from. Hedonists like the French knew a thing or two
about designing the fronts of their cars, Anna thought,
and silently thanked them.

It was about three-thirty when Claire's friend emerged
blinking into the sunlight. Her wet hair was combed back
behind her ears and she looked relaxed and shiny. She
was alone. Anna felt a sudden lurch of dismay. Had
Claire gone already? Could she have missed her? She
should have waited inside. But the girl turned back to
peer through the glass doors and then shrugged and made
her way slowly down the ramp to the road. Claire was still
there; she would come out in a minute. Her friend was
waiting.

Anna watched the glass doors, wondering what was
holding Claire back. Probably another rendezvous, she
thought. Claire was quite capable of turning an innocent
swim with a girl-friend into a secret date with a boy-
friend.

Someone screamed. Anna turned quickly and saw
Claire's friend struggling with a man wearing a motor-

cycle helmet. The girl screamed again but the man flung
his arm across her face and dragged her backwards.

Anna glanced back at the glass doors. Where was
Claire? She turned again frantically. It took her a couple
of seconds to adjust. Was it a game?

People walked by. Some of them even stopped to stare.
Anna suddenly felt alone in a world of waxworks. Who's
going to help? A girl manhandled in the street, only yards
away, someone's got to help!

Me? Better move or it'll be too late.

'Help!' yelled Anna, almost paralysed by her own
stupidity. She raced towards the struggle.

Two men burst from a van. They wore crash helmets
with dark visors and they weren't coming to help.

Unable to stop, she could only turn her impetus into a
charge. At the last moment she dropped her right
shoulder and cannoned into one of the men, hitting him
in the solar plexus. He let out a retching cough and his
helmet flew off as they both went sprawling in the gutter.

'Shit!' he gasped.

'Help!' screeched Anna, struggling to her feet. But
someone rammed a black dustbin liner over her head and
shoulders. She couldn't breathe. Her arms were pinned to
her sides and she was yanked off her feet. She kicked
backwards as hard as she could.

'Help!' shouted the man who was carrying her.

'Help!' screamed Anna wildly through the plastic.

Someone grabbed her feet and she was slung like a bag
of rubbish into the back of a van. It felt like a rugby
scrum in there. A weight crashed into the middle of her
back.

'Move, move, move!' someone yelled. Doors slammed
and the van jerked away. Everyone was cursing and
tumbling about.

'Throw her out, you berk!'

'Christ! Where'd she come from?'

'What're we going to do? We got to get rid of her!'

'We can't, you fucking pillock! She clocked me!'

Anna panicked. She heaved herself up, trying to tear the clinging plastic away from her face. For a moment there was pandemonium, then a crunching blow on the back of her neck and she fell head first into blackness.

CHAPTER 7

Bernie was dozing on his patio with a glass of iced tea at his side, when his wife called him to the phone.

'Hello, Bern.' It was Johnny. 'Listen, mate, there's something up. Claire Fourie was brought home in a police car half an hour ago, but Anna hasn't turned up yet. I've got a nasty feeling in my water.'

'Oh Lord!' Bernie said. 'Well, I'd better come over. Have you rung the office?'

'There's no one there. I've rung his nibs' private number too and there's no answer.'

'Keep trying. He's not gone away this weekend, I know that. See if you can raise Beryl. She'll know where he is.'

'OK.' Johnny didn't sound as chipper as he normally did. 'When can you get here, chum? I don't like this at all.'

'Quick as I can. Can you tell which station the police are from?'

'St John's Wood, I think. I've seen one of the DCs somewhere.'

'Right,' Bernie said. 'I'll see you.'

Someone said, 'For Christ's sake, get up, will you?'

Anna had not realized she was not up. She looked down and saw two denim-covered knees resting on cobblestones. No feet.

She said, 'What's happening?' And a split second later someone said, 'What's happening?' like an echo, far away.

Anna said, 'Eh?'

'Eh?' said the echo. Someone was taking the micky. She turned her head to catch him at it and vomited on to the cobblestones.

A balding man in a Fair Isle cardigan sat down heavily on the plastic chair beside Bernie.

'Bernard, me old flower!' he said, blotting sweat from his upper lip with a frayed cuff. 'I didn't know it was you or I wouldn't have kept you.'

'Hello, Drew,' Bernie said, looking at his watch. He had been waiting in an interview room for over an hour and a half. 'I didn't expect to see you in this neck of the woods. Limehouse, wasn't it?'

'Yeah, well, they keep pushing me sideways. Never up, mind you. So, you went private after all, that right? What's it like?'

'Fair to middling,' Bernie murmured. 'Look, what's the info on this kidnapping? Miss Lee is a colleague of mine.'

'Yes, well, tricky this one,' Drew said, blowing out his cheeks. 'I don't know what I should say. We're supposed to keep buttoned, as you well know.'

'I've got to tell her relatives something,' Bernie said patiently. Drew, he remembered, had always been strong on self-importance.

'Well, seeing as you're almost trade yourself, I suppose it won't matter. Of course we'd appreciate a little tit for tat.'

'Of course,' Bernie said amiably. 'For instance?'

'For instance, what was your girl doing on Verity Hewit's heels? It rather changes the complexion when one of yours turns up right smack on a hot-spot, doesn't it? Rather changes the complexion.' Drew savoured the words. He had probably just heard them upstairs.

'We weren't interested in Verity Hewit,' Bernie said slowly. 'Just Claire Fourie. A custody case, the father's got a bee in his bonnet. But there's nothing there. We were dropping it anyway, come Tuesday.'

'Straight up?'

'Straight up,' Bernie said levelly. 'You could ask your chief super to get on to my governor for the details. But it's a non-starter.'

'Well, if you say so, mate,' Drew said dubiously, adding with pomposity, 'Your firm's always been on the up-and-up so far as we know. But they'll have my liver for hors d'œuvres if there's any cock-up.'

Bernie sighed. He knew that Drew would not be talking to him now if the conversation had not already been approved by his superiors. He said, 'No sweat, Drew. My boss and yours are probably in pow-wow right now. The old man has chums under all the best carpets.' From the look on Drew's face, he saw he was probably right.

Drew said, 'That Claire Fourie's a proper little cracker. It can't have been much like hard work keeping a peeled eye on her.'

'Do me a favour,' Bernie protested lightly while his fists clenched unseen beneath the table. 'I've got kids of my own older than that. What did she have to say, though? She was there, wasn't she?'

'Oh, she was there all right. But she wasn't much help. And neither was that other bunch of prannies. Witnesses, I ask you. There were four of them, everyone says, but they all had crash helmets on with visors down. Leather jackets and jeans too, the uniform, you know. Apparently your girl had a go at one of them and knocked his helmet off. Unlucky really. If it weren't for that they'd've like as not left her behind.'

'Yes,' Bernie said, 'but did anyone get a face?'

'Well, we've been showing them the books, natch, and

some women picked out a mug, so we thought we were
getting somewhere, but it turns out the mug they picked
has been tucked up in Brixton for eighteen months.'

'Not out on parole or anything?'

'Locked up tighter than a fish's arse.'

'Anyone I know?'

'After your time, I should think. A young villain called
Morris Natt.'

'I'm not that well genned up on the young ones,' Bernie
agreed, just to grease the wheels. 'What's he like?'

'Bit of a floater, works for all sorts. Lives with his mum
in Camberwell. A bit dim. He was done for assault with a
dangerous weapon and possession of stolen property,
etcetera, etcetera, after some blague in Fulham.' Drew
was enjoying himself. He had probably just got the
information himself.

'How about Verity Hewit?'

'Can't tell you much there,' Drew said reluctantly, his
small triumph receding. 'The old man's got an antique
shop. That's about all that's known at present. We've got
people over there now.'

'Of course,' Bernie said, 'but he's not wealthy or
famous or anything like that?'

'Not that I've heard.'

'Or bent?'

'No.'

'What about the mother?'

'So far as I know she's just a common or garden
housewife.'

'Oh well,' Bernie sighed, disappointed.

'We'll turn something up, never you fear,' Drew said
complacently. 'We always do.'

With an effort Anna lifted her eyelids. She felt her eyes
rolling loosely in their sockets and she couldn't focus. 'I
feel sick,' she said, but her voice sounded like a horse

neighing in an echo-chamber, so she closed her eyes again
and swam back into the dark.

'So, what do we know?' Mr Brierly asked briskly. He,
Johnny and Bernie had gathered in his office. Anna's
shoulder-bag lay on the desk between them. It was late
evening.

'The girl is Verity Hewit,' Bernie said. 'From the same
school as Claire. There were four men involved, or maybe
five, the witnesses couldn't be sure. They think the driver
may have stayed put. Apparently, Anna appeared from
nowhere and knocked one of the men down. Then she
was thrown in the back of a navy-blue Bedford Transit
with Verity and driven away.'

'The Transit's turned up already,' Johnny put in. 'Near
Archway. Stolen. No dabs.'

'There were two women who say they got a quick look
at one of the men,' Bernie went on. 'They were all
wearing crash helmets but his got knocked off. When the
St John's Wood people showed the women the mug book,
they picked out Morris Natt. They said they were quite
definite about it, but when the police rang round they
found he was already banged up in Brixton.'

'And no one else saw anything?' Brierly asked.

'No,' Johnny told him bitterly. 'A few people say they
heard the rumpus, and a couple of them say they saw the
van pull away. But these two old girls are the only ones
who'll admit anything out of the ordinary happened at
all.'

'Except Claire,' Bernie added. 'But she wasn't much
help. Too far away, she says.'

'That's somewhat ironical,' Mr Brierly said stiffly.
'More than that, it's embarrassing. Now, what about
Verity Hewit? Why was she abducted?'

'Nobody seems to know,' Bernie said. 'In fact, the
police are inclined to think it's a mistake. Her father's an

antique dealer, not particularly wealthy.'

'Antiques?' Brierly raised his eyebrows.

'Kosher, so far as anyone knows,' Bernie said. 'But it's worth a look. And another thing, there've been no demands.'

'You don't suppose it's something Claire's father cooked up?' Johnny asked. 'And the boys he hired grabbed the wrong girl?'

'I don't think we can admit that as a possibility,' Brierly said. 'Unbalanced as he may be, he would hardly organize the abduction of someone who was already under surveillance.'

'No,' Bernie agreed, 'but the police are checking on him anyway. I'm afraid I had to give them quite a full account of what Anna was doing there. Her identity card was in her bag.'

'Never mind that,' Brierly said. 'Now, who knew the girls were going swimming?'

'Claire's mother and Verity's mother,' Johnny said. 'Apparently Claire swears she told nobody else.'

'But?'

'But there's always the boy she's been seeing.'

'And we still don't know who he is, do we? Have you spoken to him yet?'

'No,' Johnny said. 'He and the others who slept at his place last night left at about midday. And none of them have been back since.'

'Anything else?' Brierly asked. 'Anything at all?'

'Well,' Bernie said slowly. 'It's funny those two old birds should be so sure about Morris Natt. I'd like to talk to someone about that.'

'I see. Well, you might like to follow it up,' Brierly said. 'It's not much but we've got to do something. And, Mr Crocker, I'd like you to stay in touch with the Fouries. Talk to Claire if you can, and try to track her boy-friend down.'

'Anna took a couple of snaps of him on the Heath,' Bernie remembered. 'The film should still be in the camera. We didn't bother to get it developed, bearing in mind the way things were shaping up.'

'Well, you could see to that, too,' Brierly said. 'And if this fellow doesn't appear again, one of you should get hold of the lease-holder. She may know who he is.'

'Right,' Johnny said, 'is that it?'

'For the time being,' Brierly said, staring at his notes. 'I shall be here all day tomorrow, of course. And then there's the little matter of notifying Miss Lee's family.'

'I'll handle that, shall I?' Bernie suggested quickly.

'I'd be most grateful, Mr Schiller,' Brierly said formally, looking down at his hands.

CHAPTER 8

The fuzzy yellow orb above her head became a light-bulb. Someone was timidly shaking her foot.

Anna pulled her foot away and tried to sit up but her right arm was firmly attached to something behind her head, and her head seemed to be attached to nothing.

'Who hit me?' she asked muzzily.

'Oh, do try and wake up,' the girl at the other end of the bed said miserably. 'You've been unconscious for ages. I thought you were dead.' Her voice trailed away into tears.

'No such luck,' Anna mumbled thickly. 'Is there any water?'

'No, and we're both tied up.'

'That explains it,' Anna said, relieved. 'I thought it was brain damage.' She twisted around, trying to ignore the pain in her head and neck. A purple hand was tied with string to the iron bedrail. She couldn't feel it, but it appeared to be her own. The knots hadn't been tied by an expert. That was the only encouraging thing, so she set to work.

'Oh, don't do that,' the girl wailed. 'They'll be so angry.'

'Well, take your pick. It's them or me. Who are you, anyway?'

'Verity,' the girl said. 'Verity Hewit. I just don't understand what's happening.'

'Me neither.' She loosened the first knot and lay back to rest. She felt exhausted and sweat trickled down her face. 'What the hell happened?'

'Can't you remember?' Verity said desolately, as if Anna's concussion were purposely contributing to her loneliness. 'I'd been swimming with my friend Claire and I was just coming out when this man grabbed me. It was so frightening. Then you came running up.'

'I ought to mind my own business. People are always telling me that.'

'Didn't you want to save me?' Verity said tearfully.

'Oh hell, of course I did. I'm only joking to cheer myself up.' Anna squinted along the bed. Verity was huddled at the other end, bowed and very uncomfortable. Her hair was in rat-tails, and it looked as if traces of vomit were clinging to the ends near her face.

'How old are you?' Anna said gently.

'Fifteen. Everyone thinks I'm older because I'm so tall for my age.' She was acting a lot younger, Anna thought, but guessed that she had been frightened silly. She turned her attention back to the string. At the moment, it was the easiest thing to deal with. Verity watched her fearfully. Eventually, the last knot came undone, and Anna gingerly unwound the string. She had to lower her right arm with her left hand. It was completely paralysed and numb.

'How long have we been here?' Anna asked, nursing her

arm against her chest and waiting with trepidation for the
circulation to return.

'Ages. It's been dark for hours.'

'Christ!' Anna gritted her teeth and rocked back and
forth.

'Does it hurt?' Verity's voice trembled.

'Not half,' Anna gasped. 'How's yours?'

'Oh, not that bad really. I can move it a bit and it's not
blue like yours. They were much rougher with you. You
made them ever so angry.'

'Good,' Anna said through clenched teeth. She started
to swear monotonously, but stopped when she saw
Verity's frightened face.

In the end, the pain eased, and she was able to take
more notice of their surroundings. They were on a
chipped iron bed; the mattress was scarred with cigarette
burns. On the floor, near Verity, was a yellow plastic
bowl. Verity had been sick in it, and it looked as though
she had peed as well. High on one wall was a shallow
rectangular window. It was out of reach and had bars
across it. In another whitewashed brick wall was a solid
door. That was about all. The forty-watt bulb gave a
weak yellow light and did nothing to illuminate the dark
corners.

'What a hole,' Anna sighed. 'Now let's get you untied.'

'Oh, please don't,' Verity pleaded. 'Honestly, I'm all
right. They said they'd kill me if I tried to get away.'

'Don't be daft,' Anna said. 'You can't stay like that.'
She put her good arm around the girl's shoulder. 'Come
on, I won't let anyone hurt you.' Verity burst into tears.

'It's OK,' Anna said, rocking her awkwardly. 'No one'll
blame you.' Verity cried even harder, but allowed Anna
to untie her hand. The string was quite loose anyway and
Verity could easily have done it herself if she had had the
courage. Anna rolled up both pieces of string and put
them in her pocket. When you have nothing, everything

seems valuable, she thought, and got shakily to her feet. Of course the door wouldn't budge, but in the corner beside it was a bucket of water.

'Thank God for that,' she said, carrying it over to the bed. She drank several handfuls and encouraged Verity to do the same. She looked for her bag. She couldn't remember dropping it, but it was missing.

'What happened to your swimming things?' she asked. They found them under the bed; a damp towel, a wet Speedo and a comb.

'Wonderful,' Anna said and dipped a generous corner of the towel into the water. She wiped Verity's face and hands with it, and cleaned her hair as well as she could. Her whole face was swollen with crying and she looked as weary as death.

'Come on, love,' Anna said when she was finished, 'lie down and get a bit of kip. It won't be so bad in the morning.'

She carried the evil-smelling bowl over to the door and used it herself, embarrassed by Verity's gaze, but too tired and ill to care.

'I'm cold,' Verity said from the bed.

'That's OK. We'll keep each other warm.' She lay down and Verity put her head on her shoulder. Anna put an arm round her. There wasn't much else to do, and although she was keyed up and anxious herself, she knew that both of them needed sleep more than anything.

CHAPTER 9

Bernie fumbled with the intricacies of Beryl's switchboard and at last succeeded in dialling his home number. When his wife answered, he said, 'Hello, Syl, it's me.'

'Hello, pet,' Sylvia said warmly. 'Is there any more news?'

'No,' he said. 'No, not yet.'

'Oh, poor Anna!' she exclaimed. 'And poor you. Are you coming home now?'

'Not yet.' Bernie fingered the knot of his tie. 'Did you get Bill?'

'Right after you called me from St John's Wood,' Sylvia told him. 'I was lucky, he's been on the canals and just got back.'

'Good girl. Could he help?'

'Well, he had to go to Criminal Records, but he phoned back about half an hour ago. I've got the address you want right here on the pad.'

'Good.' Bernie searched the desk drawer until he found Beryl's scratchpad and one of her innumerable ballpoints.

'That's the mother, Kathleen Natt, right?' he said, as a crackle drowned Sylvia's voice.

'Yes, dear, and she doesn't sound very nice,' Sylvia said warningly. 'Bill says she's got a couple of Drunk and Disorderlies against her. So be careful. I don't suppose she'll be too cooperative at this time of night anyway. Really, it'd be better if you came back and got a bit of hot supper and a good sleep. You'll be so much sharper in the morning.'

'I wish I could, Syl,' Bernie said truthfully. 'But I don't like to waste time.'

'Of course you don't,' Sylvia said soothingly. 'Well, take care and come back as soon as you can.'

Bernie grinned and hung up. Johnny had already left to go back to Belsize Park, but Mr Brierly was still in his office. Bernie went quietly downstairs. He did not want to be called back for one of Mr Brierly's little chats.

Anna awoke from a blue, clear dream of flying. It had contained something about a cleanly laundered hand-kerchief. Verity was curled beside her on the sour mattress. Nothing had changed except the light had been turned off.

She eased herself away from the bed. A thin line of light was leaking under the door. She put her eye to the keyhole but could see nothing. She thought she could hear whispering.

Verity turned over, moaning, so Anna went back to bed.

'Well, you see, just as we were leaving, I remembered I'd left my hairslide in the changing-room. Verity was going to wait in the sun.' Claire sat on a piano stool, hands folded in her lap.

'I understand you're very worried about your friend, Mr Crocker,' Mrs Fourie said gently, 'but we've been over all this with the police. I'm sure they're doing all they can.' She was wearing a pale blue cardigan that matched her eyes, and her fair hair was drawn back in a neat chignon. She looked pale and tired, but a little like Grace Kelly. Johnny liked her.

He said, 'I know, and I'm sorry. It's been a long day, but could I ask you for a cup of tea? Then I'll go.'

'Yes, of course,' she said warmly. 'You must be feeling awful. And I'm so sorry for Mrs Hewit too. I wish there was something I could do. Poor, poor little Verity.'

When she had gone, Johnny abruptly turned to Claire. 'OK, ducky,' he said quickly, 'who's the boy-friend?'

'What?' Claire's beautiful blonde hair swung across her face.

'Who are you seeing?' Johnny's voice though quiet was flat and hard. 'Was he at the pool this afternoon?'

'I don't know what you're talking about.' Claire's aquamarine eyes were blank with innocence. 'But I think you ought to go away, right now, or I'll tell Mum you're bullying me.'

'You may be Little Bo-Peep to her, ducky, but not to

me. I've seen the photos. Do you want your mum to see them, too? Or your dad?'

'You're a liar. What photos?' But she kept her voice down and looked quickly at the door.

'Having your Sunday joint on the Heath, kiddo. Remember? Washed down with a little vodka and chips. Interesting company you keep. Who is he?'

'If you think I'll tell a boring old fart like you, you're an idiot,' Claire said viciously.

'That's more like the real Claire Fourie,' Johnny said with approval. 'But it's too bad for you, dearie. I thought you liked your little secrets.'

She thought about it, glaring at him through slit eyes. 'What if I do tell?'

'You aren't the only one who can keep a secret.'

'Only, if I tell you, and you ever spilt on me, I'll make you very sorry,' she said in a thin little voice. Johnny laughed but didn't reply.

'His name is Henry Ames. Everyone calls him H.'

'And he lives downstairs,' Johnny said. 'Now isn't that sweet.'

'He moved in to be close to me.' Claire lifted her bright head contemptuously. 'You wouldn't understand.'

'How long's he been there?'

'Eleven days.'

'And before that?'

'I don't know.'

'Milk and sugar?' Janet Fourie asked, coming in with the tea tray.

'I'm tired, Mum,' Claire said, jumping up. 'I want to go to bed.'

'Go on then, dear,' Mrs Fourie said.

'Sweet dreams,' said Johnny.

Bernie found the address he was looking for after driving round and round a dark muddled area just west of Coldharbour Lane. Most of the street signs had been removed or defaced. It was a small block of flats with all the grace and elegance of an empty warehouse. Bernie parked outside and went in. Kathleen Natt lived on the ground floor and Bernie found her door with the help of his torch. The passage was unlit, either by accident or design, but he smelled the reek of tomcats and trod carefully.

He knocked softly. No one answered but he could hear music inside. He searched further with his torch and found a bell. He pressed it but there was no sound so he knocked again more loudly. A woman's voice shouted, 'What is it?'

'Kathleen?' Bernie asked.

'Is it business?' the voice asked, more interested.

'Yes,' he said, unthinking.

'Well, I'm busy now,' the voice cooed. 'Come back in about half an hour.'

Bernie ran a finger round his collar and went back to his car to wait. The road was deserted except for a cat tearing a grisly supper from the depths of a cardboard box.

After a while a man appeared at the door of the flats. He paused for a second, looking nonchalantly up and down the road. Then he turned up the collar of his jacket and walked briskly away. The cat fled. Bernie locked the car and trudged back to Kathleen Natt's door. From behind it, he could hear 'A Taste of Honey' being given the full string treatment. He knocked again.

'Who is it?' The voice sounded blurred now.

'It's me again,' Bernie said. 'Let me in.'

'Give us a chance,' the voice complained. He heard a chain being put on the door. A woman peered out. Her hair was ash-blonde and curled round her face, but her eyebrows were black and the marble-grey eyes were rimmed heavily with black mascara. She studied him for a few seconds and then closed the door to take the chain off.

'Can't be too careful,' she said as she let him in. She ushered him into a room furnished with a large divan, a dressing-table and a frilly pink lampshade.

'Take your coat off, love,' she said. She stood on the other side of the bed. Bernie couldn't see her clearly in the dim pink light, but he got the impression of massive shoulders and a sagging neck inadequately covered by a scarlet rayon kimono.

'CIA,' she said without enthusiasm.

'Sorry?'

'Cash In Advance,' she snapped, making money movements with her fingers.

'Oh,' Bernie said, reaching for his wallet. 'How much?' She hesitated, looking him over carefully. 'Twenty quid,' she suggested brightly.

'Give over,' Bernie protested. 'I don't want to stay all night.'

'Fifteen. Take it or leave it,' she said. 'I want a drink. Think it over.' She walked out, and Bernie heard the sound of bottle on glass from the next room. He followed her into a sitting-room, and caught her raising what looked like a tumbler full of neat gin to her mouth. She moved quickly so that a coffee table was between them.

'I don't want you in here,' she said angrily.

'It's all right,' Bernie said. 'I just want to talk.'

'That's extra,' she said, unmollified, 'and I still don't want you in here.'

Bernie looked around. The small room was bursting with a three piece suite covered in beige nylon fur. The curtains were beige too and covered with emerald green triffids fighting for supremacy. There was a television with a twenty-four-inch screen in the corner and a heavy oak sideboard against the wall opposite the window. Everything was too big and too fussy. The blue budgerigar hanging on an ornate stand by the sideboard seemed to think so too. He sat in the sand on the bottom of his cage in a state of deep depression.

'What's wrong with your budgie?' Bernie asked, going over to look.

'He's a bit off colour, like me,' Kathleen said. 'Now, out!' She moved again so that now the sofa was between them. Bernie didn't blame her. She plied a risky trade and didn't take more chances with strangers than she had to.

The sideboard was covered with china mugs, souvenirs from the seaside and mementoes of royal occasions. There were also numerous photographs. One of them interested Bernie more than the others. It was a snap of Kathleen, taken in better days. A mini-skirt half-covered her plump thighs, and she was holding hands with two small boys. One was older than the other, but they looked alike. Underneath was written in careful but graceless letters, 'Morry, Gary and Me. Aug. 1965.'

'These your boys?' Bernie asked, picking the photo up.

'Leave it be. That's private,' Kathleen said furiously.

'They're fine boys,' Bernie said.

'Well, they grew up, didn't they,' she said. Her tone of voice implying that boys were one thing, but men were all the same.

'Do you see much of them now?'

'Look, that's my affair, ennit?' Kathleen was very drunk and very angry. 'Now what about the business? Do you want it or don't you? I'm getting fed up of you in here bunnying where you don't belong.'

'Sorry,' Bernie said quietly. 'Like I said, I just wanted a chat, I didn't mean to upset you.' He took a fiver out of his wallet and laid it on the sideboard. 'I'll be off now. I don't want to waste your time.'

He left her glowering on the other side of the mountainous furniture and let himself out into the dark passage. He went to his car, and stood for a minute looking back at the dark flats. Then he let his breath out slowly with relief. It was two in the morning and he needed to sleep. But at least he had something to do when he woke up.

Screaming. Someone was screaming. Anna leapt to her feet in the dark and staggered, off balance, against a wall. She was sick and giddy. The screams turned to growling moans. She crouched down because she thought she was going to fall. Her head was spinning, she trembled with chilly sweat and spasms of nausea rose to the back of her throat.

Verity turned over and mumbled in her sleep. Anna's head cleared slowly. It's cats, she told herself. And then, it's concussion. In fact, it was both. The growls tightened into screams again: cats fighting. She sighed and waited till she felt stronger and could tiptoe to the buckets by the door. By the time she got there, she didn't want to be sick anymore, so she sipped some water to settle her stomach and went back to bed.

Verity had rolled over into the middle so Anna lay on the edge grateful for the warmth of the other body. She had to sleep, she told herself. Then she would feel better and be able to get herself and Verity out of the mess they were in. She couldn't think now. Sleep was the only answer. But every time her eyes closed, she teetered on the edge of a nightmare and had to fight her way back to consciousness. Suppose she did get to sleep and then never woke up? She had heard of that happening to people who had been concussed. Or suppose she went to sleep and woke up blind? Or suppose those blokes in crash helmets were insane? Or suppose you give it a rest now, she told herself sternly, it's worse than useless you getting yourself stewed up now. She tried to think about Bea and Selwyn's cistern. Sometimes it wouldn't fill, and she had promised to have a look at it for them. Mentally, she took the plumbing apart, and gradually, as she did so, she calmed down and her heart stopped racing.

CHAPTER 10

Anna woke to a surly grey morning. She looked at her wrist but her watch had stopped at five o'clock. Verity wasn't wearing one. Anna got cautiously to her feet and experimented with her arms and legs. They seemed to be working as usual although she was stiff and cold. Her head still felt like an old golf-ball but at least her balance was normal again. Verity was still asleep. Anna squatted over the slop bucket, glad to be unobserved. She didn't think she was excessively modest, it was just that there were some things you got used to doing in private. She hoped she wouldn't have the time to get used to an audience. There was no toilet-paper. Small things like that were going to become demoralizing if she couldn't find some way to get herself and Verity released quickly. There was a piece of Kleenex tucked in her sleeve. She tore it in half. One piece of Kleenex wouldn't go very far. She stood up. Her clothes smelled terrible so she undressed and scrubbed herself with a damp corner of the towel.

'I'm hungry,' Verity complained as she woke up.

Anna pulled her shirt back on and buttoned it up. She had washed as thoroughly as she could. She gave Verity the towel.

'Have a drink of water,' she said. 'It'll fill you up a bit.'

'Do you think they're just going to leave us here?' Verity asked, drinking and splashing water on her face.

'There was someone around last night,' Anna told her. Verity looked much better this morning. She was a large, healthy-looking girl, taller than Anna, but with shy brown eyes and a diffident way of holding herself. She seemed surprised and troubled by the size of her body as if she had grown very quickly and hadn't got over the shock of it.

'Should we shout, or something?' she said, scrubbing furtively under her arms.

'Not yet,' Anna said, stripping the mattress off the bed. 'I want to have a look at the window.'

She turned to ask Verity to help her with the bed, but Verity was gazing at the slop bucket with a revolted expression on her face.

'I want to go to the loo,' she said in a small voice.

'I've only got half a tissue,' Anna said, handing it to her. 'You'll just have to hold your nose. It can't be helped.' She turned her back politely and started heaving at the iron bedstead. After a while Verity came and gave her a hand.

'Do you think you'd better?' she said, pulling worriedly at her fingers. 'Suppose you got caught?'

'I'd feel even more of a fool if I sat here doing nothing, when there might be a simple way out of here.'

They stood the bed on end under the window, and Verity steadied it while Anna clambered on top. The sill was just level with her chin if she stood on tiptoe. Even so, the window was sunk six inches below ground level and all she could see, looking up through the murky panes, was a brick wall about nine feet away. The bars were on the other side of the glass. They were eight inches apart and looked sturdy. She would have to break the glass to test them.

'What can you see?' Verity asked.

'Sod all,' Anna said disgustedly. 'Give me one of your shoes.' The bed wobbled dangerously as Verity took one off. She handed it to Anna. It was a rope-soled canvas shoe with not much strength to it, but she put her hand in it and attacked the glass.

'Don't look up,' she warned Verity. But it took a few minutes of steady bashing before she produced a crack. Even then, the glass didn't break properly, and she had to pick out a hole large enough to put her hand through. She tried three of the bars in the end, but they all felt firmly embedded in the wall. Besides, her stance on the shaky bed did not give her adequate leverage, so she stopped.

'Oy!' she shouted at the top of her voice. She went on shouting for ten minutes, but her voice seemed to fall dead against the silence. Only the distant traffic noise told her that they were close to something.

'Your turn,' she said hoarsely, climbing down at last.

'Do I have to?' Verity said. 'What if one of them comes?'

'Suit yourself,' Anna said. 'But, if one of them was here, they'd've come in by now, and we'd be barmy not to take the chance while we're alone.'

While Verity was shouting at the window, Anna examined the bed. It was an old-fashioned iron construction with criss-crossed springs. She thought that with a bit of effort she could work one of the springs loose. Then, if she could straighten it out a bit, she might have a crack at the lock.

Bernie ate scrambled eggs and tomatoes for breakfast. He sat in the warm kitchen with his daughter while Sylvia made tea and more toast than either of them could finish. His daughter knew she had until August to wait for her A-level results. But she had refused to go away that summer and anxiously examined the post every morning. She expected catastrophe in every envelope. Bernie smiled at her sympathetically. He thought that she had probably done very well. She had been like a horse on hot cobbles about her O-levels too, but even the excellence of those results hadn't given her confidence.

His two sons, both at university, were spending the summer in Israel. They had been very successful in exams, but neither of them worried like his daughter.

Bernie allowed himself a quiet moment of satisfaction. Not bad for an old copper, he thought. He hadn't had much formal schooling himself but believed whole-heartedly in the benefits of a good education. All the same, he knew there was nothing like a happy childhood. The kids had been bright and eager to learn, but also cheerful and so he counted himself lucky. Sylvia caught him smiling and smiled too. They had all been lucky, he told himself. Good ideas and good management were all very fine but you needed to be fortunate as well.

'What are you going to do now?' Sylvia asked. He had already rung the office to see if there was any news. There wasn't. But Johnny had found the lease-holder of the basement flat and was on his way to Hampstead to find her. Bernie had also phoned Drew at St John's Wood station with the information that Morris Natt had a younger brother who resembled him, but he had been given a polite but definite brush-off. This did not surprise or wound him in the least. He knew how people on the inside felt about those on the outside. He had been on the inside once himself and understood the feelings of superiority and self-sufficiency.

'I think I'll go and see Bessy Corde,' he replied slowly. 'She was a good contact once. I shouldn't think she's all that close to the action anymore. She went very respect-able after her second marriage. But she's still got the pub, as far as I know, and she used to know everything and everyone.'

'Will she talk to you?' Sylvia asked.

'She loves a good gossip, does Bessy,' Bernie told her. 'Besides, she was never a hard nark, so to speak. More a genealogist. You know, all the family trees and background stuff. If she doesn't know the Natts herself, she'll know someone who does.'

'Well, I hope you're right,' Sylvia said, 'and I hope someone comes up with something quickly. I don't even like to think what's happening to Anna.'

'What *is* happening to Anna?' their daughter asked, dragging herself out of her own anxieties.

'Ask your mother,' Bernie said, fondly ruffling her hair. 'I've got to get going.'

Greta Hall had curly orange hair. She wore a mauve and white patterned dress of Indian cotton, and leather sandals.

'Are you the fuzz?' she said, looking up from the photographs Johnny had given her.

She was forty-five if she was a day, he thought. 'No, no,' he said affably. 'I'm just looking for a friend.'

'I see,' she said, lighting a cigarette. 'Then which one of these people is your friend, and how come you have this photograph? It looks as though it was taken with a telephoto lens.'

She wasn't as silly as she looked, Johnny thought. 'None of them,' he said. 'She took the picture.'

Greta took a deep pull at her cigarette and exhaled slowly. 'Then she's known to the people in this group?' She looked as if she was enjoying herself.

'Not exactly, no,' Johnny said, thoroughly discomfited. It had all looked so simple ten minutes ago.

'Do you really expect me to answer questions about my friends simply because you choose to ask them? Kids have to put up with too much harassment these days. You wave an extremely suspicious-looking photograph under my nose and expect me to inform on my friends to someone I've never met before.'

Johnny sighed and reached for his identity card. 'I'd better start at the beginning,' he said.

When he had finished, she lit another cigarette. 'So you just want to find this Henry Ames to see if he has any connection with the kidnapping? And you are not the fuzz? And you have no intention of talking to them about drugs on the Heath?'

'That's right,' Johnny said. 'I give you my word.'

'OK then, you'd better talk to Mark.' She indicated one of the young men in the picture.

'Where can I find him?' Johnny asked.

'Upstairs,' Greta said sweetly, 'he's my son.' She went to the bottom of the stairs and called up, leaving Johnny with his mouth open.

He was sitting in the kitchen of the house Anna had failed to find three days ago. The window overlooked a garden completely given over to growing vegetables. Beyond the wall was Parliament Hill. The kitchen was warm and spicy. Bottle-green paint couldn't disguise the elegant moulding on the walls and high ceiling, and the proportions of the room dwarfed the pine furniture decorating it. In fact, it was a room which altogether defied the cottage mentality that had tried to shape it.

Johnny sighed again. He should have been warned by the untidy heaps of *Guardians*, *Times Literary Supplements* and *Private Eyes*.

Mark Hall, when he came in, was wearing a scarlet happi-coat with black Japanese characters all over it and that was all. The coat was very short and the sight of Mark's long slim legs made Johnny uncomfortable.

'Clever,' Mark said, picking up the photograph. 'I didn't know anyone was following us. It's not a bad picture, is it? What sort of lens was she using?' Far from being outraged, Mark seemed to feel flattered.

'A two-fifty, I think,' Johnny began, unprepared.

'Must have supported it on her knee,' Mark went on, 'the picture's very sharp for such a distance. I do a bit of photography at Reading,' he explained. 'So you want to do a bird-dog on poor old H, do you? Well, if he's not at the flat, I don't know where you'll find him.'

'When did you see him last?'

'Must have been Saturday,' Mark said vaguely. 'Yes, because we all crashed there on Friday night.' He winked at his mother. 'Had a bit too much to drink or something.'

'That's why I kept the lease,' Greta said, as if she were just getting proof that some obscure policy was being vindicated. 'People need somewhere to let off steam.'

'And you haven't seen him since?' Johnny asked, ignoring her.

'No, we came back here for lunch and then he went off somewhere. I didn't ask,' he added.

'What about the others, would they know?'

'Shouldn't think so. H is a bit of an outlaw, doesn't say much. Claire should know, though. She's his bird.'

'Mark!' Greta said sharply.

'Sorry, Greta,' Mark said, this time winking at Johnny. 'She doesn't like me demeaning women.'

'Claire isn't a woman. She's only fourteen.'

'Jesus!' Johnny had the satisfaction of seeing Mark's complacent face fall. 'I didn't know that.'

'Why not? You've got the flat under hers. Didn't you introduce her to H?'

'The other way round. I don't go there much, and I certainly don't remember ever seeing her.'

'Go on. Tell me about it.'

'Well, it's funny really. I came down from Reading about a week ago. With Sandy. That's him in the picture. And we went round to the flat with Sandy's girl-friend. I was thinking of giving him the key. They don't have anywhere to go, if you know what I mean. Well, we opened the door and walked in, and there was H eating Marmite sandwiches. I mean, really. He lives on Marmite. It seemed sort of amusing, me having a

squatter. After all, I've lived in a squat or two at
university and I know what it's like. So of course I said he
could stay. It was a gas, really. He was carrying on this
Romeo and Juliet affair with Claire, and nobody knew he
was there. We met her later, and, well, you could see
what he was on about.'

He glanced apologetically at his mother, but she didn't
comment.

Johnny said, 'So, as far as you know, he has no other
address?'

'Of course not. He'd hardly bother to squat if he had.'

'I don't know about that,' Johnny said. 'Does he have
any friends?'

'Not that I know of. Except that chap at Charing Cross.
No, he's a loner. His family threw him out when he
couldn't find a job, and he's lived hand to mouth ever
since. Quite heroic, really.'

'What chap at Charing Cross?'

'Well, not a friend even. H seemed to know him, that's
all. He sells tea off a van, and hamburgers.'

'At Charing Cross?'

'Not the main line, but under the railway bridge
opposite the Underground. There's an arcade. H has a
thing about Space Invaders, and we went there one
afternoon to play the machines. He's quite an eccentric.
It was hours before we could drag him away.'

'And that's all you know about him?' Johnny said
wonderingly. 'He likes Marmite and Space Invaders and
has a mate who sells tea?'

'What do you know about anyone?' Greta said tartly.
'Have you finished now? I want to get lunch.'

Johnny walked down the hill to his car wordlessly
defaming N.W.3. and everyone who lived there. As he
reached the car, he saw Claire coming up towards him so
he stopped and waited.

She would have passed him without recognition,

looking tired and thoughtful, but he said, 'Hello, Claire. He's not there, you know.'

She turned her deep-sea eyes on him and dragged the impudence back into her expression. 'Oh, it's you again. Still poking your nose in. Well, you won't find him.'

'Nor will you,' Johnny said.

'Who says I want to?' she said haughtily. But she must have felt the act slipping, because she turned away quickly and walked off up the hill.

CHAPTER 11

'Why didn't you come out together?' Anna asked. She was crouched on the floor trying to straighten out one of the bed-springs, using the weight of the bed as a vice. Verity was sitting on the bed as ballast.

'Claire met a friend,' she said, 'so she was saying goodbye. Claire's very popular you know.'

'Boy-friend?' Anna persisted.

'I'm not supposed to say,' Verity said, pulling at her fingers. Anna had come to know this as a symptom of anxiety.

'Who am I going to tell?' she said patiently.

'Well, she's got this boy-friend,' Verity told her, 'but nobody's supposed to know. Her family'd go wild if they found out.'

'And he went swimming with you?' Anna prompted. Talking to Verity was heavy going. She answered questions all right, but didn't seem able to carry on a conversation.

'He came later,' Verity said. 'Actually, I was ready to get out and then he turned up. So we stayed a bit longer. I might as well have gone home then. He only talked to Claire.'

'Who is he? Had you met him before?'

'No, but Claire talks a lot about him. She calls him H. I don't know his real name.'

'What does she say about him?'

'Well, that he's the real thing. He's real working class, you know, not pretend. And he's had a hard life. He doesn't approve of the bourgeoisie, but he's in love with Claire.'

'I see,' Anna said in what she hoped was a neutral tone of voice.

'They sleep together, you know,' Verity said defiantly.

'Yes?' Anna said. 'How long has she known him?'

'I know what you're thinking.' Verity looked down.

'No, you don't,' Anna said. 'I'm thinking that someone fingered you. And I was wondering if it was H or Claire.'

'It couldn't be Claire,' Verity said, shocked. 'We've been friends for ages.'

'OK. Then who else knew where you'd be yesterday afternoon?'

'Only Mum and Mrs Fourie.'

'You didn't tell anyone else?'

'I only just got back from a week at my gran's,' Verity explained. 'Claire was the first person I rang up.'

'Whose idea was it?'

'Claire's. She had a new bikini she wanted to show me. But I don't know,' she added with sudden insight, 'if it was me she really wanted to show. She wasn't very friendly. Perhaps she only took me because her mother doesn't let her go swimming on her own.'

'Moody, is she?' Anna said with sympathy. Verity looked very sad indeed.

'A bit. Only I'm used to it now.' Verity squirmed slightly and milked her fingers again. 'Oh God!' she suddenly exploded. 'This is awful. I've got to go to the loo again and I hate going in that bowl with you here. I don't know how you can be so *ordinary* about it.'

'It just can't be helped,' Anna tried to comfort her. 'There's no other way to be.'

'Suppose they come in while I was going?' All Verity's anxieties burst to the surface. 'I think they're just going to let us starve. It must be way after lunch-time, and there's hardly any water left. I'm so hungry.'

Anna tried to take the worries one at a time. She said, 'Well, don't get too steamed up, love. We'll hear them coming long before they get here. And you must be useful to them, so they're not going to let you starve or die of thirst.'

'Well, when are they coming?' Verity cried unanswerably.

Anna had nothing to say. After all, if a kidnap went wrong it was not unknown for the victims to be either killed or abandoned. She had no information about how their own kidnap was succeeding, but from what she had seen of their captors she did not have much confidence that anything was going to plan, if indeed there was a plan. It looked to her like a hopeless cock-up.

These were not the right thoughts to share with Verity though, so she just said, 'They'll come soon enough. It's Sunday, after all. Everything's late on a Sunday.'

It was a stupid thing to say but Verity took it seriously. Verity, Anna thought, would probably try to turn any silly statement into comfort. It wasn't really surprising. Time, place, and emotional state had a lot to do with determining the significance of what you said. After all, if you are on your death-bed, any old nonsense is taken seriously, but you can't get away with the same thing down in the pub in perfect health.

The Half Moon dominated an obscure crossroads within walking distance of Battersea Bridge. Years ago, it had been affectionately referred to as Jamaica Inn because of the schemes and deals that had originated from its Public

Bar. Bernie wondered if it still deserved the sobriquet. Bessy herself had always kept to the rules and it was a good orderly pub, but something about its location and clientele had made it a useful market-place for anyone with a felonious turn of mind. It followed then that it was also a pub patronized by policemen in search of information, and at night in the crowded bar it was often difficult to tell the difference between the pursuers and the pursued as they drank and talked. Certainly Bessy treated them all alike.

As Bernie approached, a man came out carrying two unwieldy bags of rubbish. He dumped them on a pile by the kerb and went back inside. It was collection day. A refuse cart turned into the bottom of the road and slowly clanked its way towards the corner noisily digesting other people's leavings. Bernie pushed through the varnished saloon doors and into the quiet dark interior.

Bessy was wearing a pink and white housecoat with a ruffle that whorled like decorative icing from her cleavage to her fluffy pink slippers. She was idly flicking dust off a large jar of pickled eggs while the Brasso dried on the beer pumps.

'Hello, Bessy,' Bernie said, settling his weight on a bar-stool.

'Why, Mr Schiller,' said Bessy, fussing with her blue-black curls in a little gesture of surprise. 'It's been an age. I heard you retired.'

'I did, Bessy, but you know how it is.'

'Got to keep active.' Bessy nodded, her several chins joining to form a single fat collar. 'What did you do then? Join one of those security firms?'

'Something like that,' Bernie admitted. 'What about you? I heard you got married again.'

'I've got to keep my hand in too,' she said with a high girlish giggle. 'Practice makes perfect. Why should I give up now when I'm just getting the hang of it? I don't know,

Mr Schiller, but nature's got it all wrong. Just when you've learned what it's all about, you're too old to do anything.'

'Never!' Bernie said with a grin. 'You're looking better than ever.' She had never been a beauty, but she had something that made men like her.

'Well, anyway,' she said, pleased, 'he's a good man, and that's what counts. It's the company, really. I missed that.'

'But not for long,' Bernie said.

'I've been lucky.' Bessy touched the shiny wood bar and then began to polish the brass, plying the duster vigorously. Bernie watched her in silence for a minute or two. The courtesies had been honoured but he didn't want to rush. After a while he said, 'There's something happened to a friend of mine. She was snatched along with another girl. Hasn't been seen since yesterday.'

'Shame,' Bessy said sympathetically. 'You're worried, aren't you? I could see that, the minute you sat down.'

'I am,' Bernie agreed. 'No one seems to know what it's all for, you see. Everyone's in the dark. The only thing is, there was a couple of witnesses, and they both picked Morris Natt out of the mug-book.'

'Couldn't be him,' Bessy said, 'unless he's over the wall and I haven't heard.'

'He isn't,' Bernie told her. 'But I was wondering about his brother. It seemed a bit of a coincidence, two people picking Morris.'

'Little Gary?' Bessy said incredulously. 'Well, he's a lot like Morris, but no one takes him seriously. He's one of those who always fall butter-side down.'

'I don't know either of them myself.'

'Well, you wouldn't,' Bessy said. 'Younger generation. I wouldn't either, but the mother used to be a friend of mine.'

'I saw her last night,' Bernie said ruefully.

'She's come down in the world since I knew her.' Bessy glanced at him quickly and then turned her attention to a row of sparkling glasses. 'She hasn't had a lot of luck, always having to manage on her own. I don't suppose she told you much.'

'I didn't ask her much,' Bernie said. 'She wasn't in the mood for talking. It was a bit late,' he added delicately.

'Those boys haven't helped. They could of, but they didn't. Morris was always in trouble. I sometimes think it runs in families. I don't mean bad blood, more the example.'

'Yes.' Bernie nodded. 'Like plumbers' sons becoming plumbers.'

'It's hard to break the mould,' Bessy agreed philosophically, 'but there's some I wish would try. Those Natt boys, for instance. They're much too dim for that sort of thing, but they will keep on.'

'Are they freelance?' Bernie asked, 'Or working for someone?'

'I don't know about Gary, but I don't think anyone'd touch him,' she said thoughtfully. 'He was just a bit of a hooligan, last I heard. Morris, now, he worked for Willy Dutch.'

'The Lord of the Manor,' Bernie said, startled. 'I thought he was more choosy.'

'He was. The way I heard it, he wanted a patsy and he chose Morris. Poor old Morris must've thought he'd hit the big time. He's been hitting it now for eighteen months, and when he gets out, no one'll want to know. You'll see.'

'All the same,' Bernie mused, 'Willy Dutch used to be a class operator.'

'Used to be,' Bessy said. 'He's slipped since then. They're doing him for murder. Hadn't you heard?'

'Willy? Stroll on!' Bernie was really surprised. 'That's not like him.'

'No? Well, it's true,' Bessy said, enjoying Bernie's amazement. 'Things've changed in the past few years. Everybody's that bit nastier and greedier.'

'Willy was quite the little folk hero,' he recalled.

'Still is,' Bessy said virtuously, 'while there's nits like those Natt brothers around to think the sun shines out of his trousers.'

'So what's happened to his firm?' Bernie asked.

'Well, so far as I know, his boy Carl's keeping things ticking over. But I haven't heard much. There's some of them still come in here now and again, but I'm not really in the know.'

'Who is?'

'Well, you could try Davey Spoon. You knew him, didn't you? He's not been active for a while but he used to have his ear to the ground. He might've heard something about Gary too, you never can tell.'

Bernie felt as if he were opening an old book; the names of half-forgotten characters jogged his memory.

'I'll have to be opening soon,' Bessy said breaking into his thoughts. 'Why don't you stay and have one with me for old times?'

'I'd love to, Bessy,' he said, 'but I ought to get on.' Much as he liked her, Bessy had brought back the past, and he wanted to get out into the fresh air to get used to the idea that he was treading paths he thought he had left to younger men long ago.

Through her eyelashes, Anna glanced up at the window, a barred rectangle the colour of spent chewing gum. She was lying down on the shabby mattress, now back on its iron bedstead. Her exertions with the spring and the intermittent shouting at the broken window had caused a sickening headache and waves of dizzy nausea. But there was nothing left in her stomach to bring up, so she lay down weakly, bathed in clammy sweat. She knew Verity

was watching her, worriedly lacing and unlacing her
fingers. It didn't help. Anna knew she was letting her
down. What Verity needed was a strong shoulder to lean
on, whereas Anna at the moment was more like a flabby
strand of plasticine.

After a while, goaded by the fixed gaze of silently
pleading eyes, she sat up.

'Are you feeling better?' Verity asked in a small voice,
moving up the bed. 'I was afraid you were dying.'

'Silly,' Anna said, a little faintly. 'It's just the bang on
the head. I'll be OK in a minute.'

'You went all yellow,' Verity accused.

'Sorry.' Anna felt she should apologize. 'Will you bring
the water over?'

'There's hardly any left,' Verity said, going to fetch it.
She was right. Anna made do with a mouthful, leaving a
little at the bottom of the bucket. She thought about the
principle which asserted that if you only took half of what
was there, and continued to take half of what was left,
then theoretically you should never run out. What
worked in theory, she thought wryly, would still leave
them very thirsty in practice.

'Pure maths,' she murmured to herself, 'is a load of
cods.'

'What?'

'Nothing,' Anna said, but then to forestall any
questions about when they would be released, she
repeated the principle to Verity.

'That's silly,' Verity said when she had understood.
'What's the point of half a drop of water?'

'None at all,' Anna replied wearily. 'That's why I said
that in these circumstances maths is codswallop.'

'I got fifty-eight per cent in my last exam,' Verity
reminisced, 'but I don't like maths much.'

'What do you like?'

'Geography, at the moment,' Verity told her. 'We've

got a good teacher in that, and . . .'

'Sh!' Anna interrupted. 'We've got visitors.' She got to her feet. Two, no, three pairs of boots coming down twenty stairs. Verity's face paled.

One bolt was pulled, then another.

'Take it easy,' Anna said.

And finally, the key. Verity scuttled like a mouse so that both Anna and the bed were between herself and the opening door.

There were three of them: all, as Anna had remembered, wearing fake leather jackets and crash helmets. They stood in the doorway, the one in front armed with a bicycle chain. He looked aggressive and ready for trouble. The two dithering behind him looked like a sinister joke; one was over six feet tall but narrow and bony, while the other was half his height, stunted and undernourished. They smelt of nervous sweat. It might have been pathetic, but now they were actually there, all Anna could feel was anger and fear.

'Well, if it isn't Shake, Rattle, and Roll,' she said coldly. 'What kept you?'

'Shut your gob, you,' said the first one to come in.

'Your dinner,' said the tall skeletal one, still in the doorway. He threw a greasy paper packet. 'Count yourself lucky.'

Anna caught it and put it on the bed. 'Lucky?' she said contemptuously. 'What is this, an exercise in total stupidity? What if one of us gets sick? How difficult do you want to make it?'

'Who the fuck cares?' said the aggressive one whom Anna now thought of as Shake.

'You should,' Anna said. 'I take it this is an economic venture, not plain cruelty. You should protect your investment.'

'What d'you want, then?' Roll, the little one, said uncertainly.

'Food, water, blankets, just the basic minimum,' Anna said sarcastically. 'Soap, a clean bucket, and bog paper. Or is cholera part of the plan? You do have a plan, I hope.'

'We was going to do that,' Roll said placatingly.

'Shut up, you berk.' Rattle hit him from behind.

'Who broke the fucking window?' Shake said angrily.

'Who do you think? We needed some fresh air.'

'Oh yeah! I told you,' he said to Verity, 'you keep doggo or else. Didn't I tell you?'

'Yes,' Verity said. She could hardly speak and her lips looked drained.

'Well, why don't you do what you're fucking told?' He strode over and grabbed her chin. 'You don't want to make me angry, do you?'

'No.'

'Oh, very clever,' Anna said. 'Gestapo tactics on little girls. Pity there aren't any kittens for you to drown. You'd like that too.'

'Shut your mouth or I'll do it for you,' Shake shouted wildly, but he left Verity alone.

Anna turned to Roll who looked the most amenable of the three. 'Bring what I asked for,' she said, 'and you won't have any more trouble.'

When they had gone, Anna knelt by the door with her ear to the keyhole. A row was raging on the other side, but she could only catch a word or two.

'I feel sick,' Verity said. Anna went over to her.

'Lie down, love. Take a few deep breaths.'

A minute or two later, the door opened again. Roll grabbed the two buckets and withdrew clumsily. Anna and Verity waited in silence. When he came back, the slop bucket was empty and the water bucket was full.

Anna breathed a sigh of relief. 'One up, to our side,' she muttered, listening to the bolts being rammed home and the key turned.

'Why did you do it?' Verity gasped faintly when she was sure they were alone again. 'You just got them upset.'

'It'll do them good,' Anna said, still angry. Then she took hold of herself and explained, 'If we're completely passive the way they want us to be, they're quite likely to leave that stinking mess in the corner and forget the water. We've got to stand up for ourselves or they're going to neglect us something rotten.'

'I'd rather be left alone.'

'That's not what you said earlier,' Anna said sturdily. 'Now get some food down you. You must be starving.'

CHAPTER 12

'Davey's retired,' said Mrs Spoon, in the doorway, 'and he's not a well man anymore. It's his chest. We just collect our pensions now, like everyone else.'

Bernie looked over her shoulder at the bare kitchen. It was not the way he remembered Davey's home. 'Perhaps you could do with a bit of help then, Mrs Spoon,' he said. 'I won't keep him long.'

'Well, seeing as you're an old business acquaintance,' she said, showing him through to the bedroom. 'I must say, you're looking well, Mr Schiller,' she added resentfully as she opened the door.

'Hello, Mr Schiller,' Davey whispered from his chair by the window. 'I haven't seen you in donkey's years.' Davey had always whispered, but now Bernie could hear the bubbling hiss of breath in his lungs. The skin on his quick little hands clung uncertainly to the bone, and his once immaculate hair was rumpled and grey. Davey was a small man, but Bernie could remember him, smart in his blue blazer and white cotton shirts, dodging round Berwick Street market like a bantamweight.

'So you're still in the game,' he said, when Bernie had explained his business. 'Old habits die hard, don't they? Well, there's not a lot I can tell you about Gary Natt. 'Course he wanted to follow his brother into a decent firm, but no one'd have him. He's too dim to come in out of a snowstorm. Never managed more than a couple of months in Borstal. He did a tailor's in Brixton and they nicked him the very next morning wearing one of the suits. See what I mean?' Davey's laugh was like a saucepan boiling over.

'Who does he run around with?' Bernie asked.

'Ah well, there's two more silly twommits like himself, Pete Wilson and Jack Hardaker. You don't know Jack, do you? He was done for thieving a couple of years back. It was a brand new Volvo and Jack only parked it on a zebra crossing while he went and bought some fags. I haven't heard much else. They're just small fry.'

'Anyone else?' Bernie asked, smiling at the story.

'Eric Tozer. He's new in the manor.' Davey's expression changed. 'I'd tell you about him for free. I was there the night old Walter died. Walter was a pal of mine.'

'I remember Walter,' Bernie said. 'What about him?'

'Well, as you know, old Walter did some business with your side, like myself. Only he was a bit past it. Well, you know, you don't ask outright but I'd heard tell he'd put the finger on Tozer for something, and there was a spot of bother. So, one night Tozer came for him. He's a mad bastard, Tozer. Come down from Glasgow about a year ago. The sort who eats glass for bets and puts the nut on folks he don't like.' Davey grimaced.

'I heard Walter had a heart attack,' Bernie reminded him.

'He did, Mr Schiller, and so would you if you got caught in an alley with Eric Tozer.'

'What happened?'

'Well, we'd been drinking, me and Walter. In the

White Bear, it was. And then I had to go out to the karsi.
A couple of minutes later I heard someone running
through, and the window open. And Walter shouts: "You
haven't seen me, Davey!" He was over sixty, Walter was,
and fat, so it can't've been easy, him getting out the
window. Well, a second or two later, Eric Tozer kicks the
door in. It near enough fell on my head. 'Course I was just
sitting there, trousers round me ankles. Not at my best.
He's got a broken bottle, see. And he rams it up to my
nose and asks me where Walter is. If I hadn't been doing
it already, he'd've given me the tom-tits. He's bleeding
mental, Mr Schiller. Anyway he didn't wait for an
answer, and he went through the window without
opening it. Glass everywhere. I heard him, outside,
shouting and Walter screaming.

'Well, I got myself together and went out there. There
was quite a few went as well, and we found poor old
Walter by the bins. He looked as if he'd tried to climb the
wall. All his fingernails was tore off. We carried him back
in, but he was in a bad way already, and he croaked in
the back bar before the ambulance came.'

'Nasty,' Bernie said softly.

'You can say that again,' Davey whispered. 'Of course,
there was questions asked, but Tozer swore he'd never
laid a finger on him, and you couldn't prove otherwise.
Who cares about a poor old snout anyway? He just wasn't
fast enough on his feet, was he? I got out, myself, soon
after. Well, it made me think, didn't it. I'm no spring
chicken myself and your lot don't look after us as they
used to. I could've got careless like old Walter, and I
didn't want to end up all of a heap by the dustbins too.'

'That won't happen to you,' Bernie said.

'No? Well, maybe not now, but it's not a game for old
traders like me anymore.' Davey looked out of the
window on to his bit of yard with its disused coal bunker
and lavatory that should have been torn down long ago.

The sight seemed to restore him.

'Who got grabbed, Mr Schiller?' he said. 'It's not like you to go whistling in the wind.'

'No,' Bernie agreed. 'It's a fifteen-year-old, Verity Hewit, and a friend of mine who went to help her.'

'Hewit?' Davey said speculatively. 'If she's related to Roly Hewit, I might be able to help you. He's appearing for your lot against Willy Dutch. You've been gone a long time or you'd've heard. Roly Hewit could drop Willy for a life.

'In the old days people used to bring Roly bits of this and that. He was always very reliable, gave a fair price and never opened his mouth. Then about fifteen years ago he went legit. Bought a little shop up in Camden and kept his nose clean. Well, one day last year Reub Irving goes to see him, so the story goes, and asks can he shift some stuff. Roly says sorry he's out of all that now and sees Reub off the premises. He's watching him go, when all of a sudden a sodding great Merc comes roaring up and rolls Reub all over the road. So Roly, not knowing any better, notes the number and phones the police. He thought it was a hit and run, see. Only it turns out the Merc belongs to Willy Dutch and it was found in Willy Dutch's garage with bits of Reub still stuck to the front bumper.'

'Reub Irving was freelancing?'

'Not even that, Mr Schiller, he'd got some of the firm's takings under his coat.'

'I don't know,' Bernie said reflectively. 'Willy and Reub were like father and son, the way I remember.'

'Speaking of which,' Davey wheezed, 'it's Willy's son Carl that's holding the fort till Willy's case goes one way or the other.'

'That's funny too,' Bernie said. 'The way I remember it, Willy sent Carl to a really good school just so's he'd be out of the business and start out well.'

'Brought him up really posh,' Davey agreed. 'Well, he

could afford to, couldn't he? Only things went wrong when the lad tried to get into university. Oh, he was clever all right but not clever enough. Willy had been right proud of him up till then. He was a great believer in education, he was. Well, they was both disappointed.'

'What happened then?' Bernie asked.

'I don't know for sure,' Davey said. 'That was about two years back when I had my first spell in hospital. But it seems that Carl did a course in business management. And the business he had in mind to manage was his dad's. There was a bit of a falling out, I heard. It only goes to show: you can't make silk purses out of sow's ears.'

'Oh, I wouldn't put it like that,' said Bernie, thinking of his own children. 'Still, it must've caused friction.'

'You're not wrong,' Davey said. 'Some of Willy's associates weren't too well pleased. A lot of them's getting on now, like Willy himself, and they don't take too kindly to a young sprig with a la-di-dah accent telling them what's what. But there's others think it's a good idea.'

'So, all in all, things are breaking up a bit,' Bernie remarked.

'Well, that's the story, for what it's worth,' Davey said tiredly. 'But it's not going to help you find the Natt boy. You see, it'd make more sense if you was looking for one of Willy's boys.'

'It would,' Bernie said. 'But it's Gary I'm after and he's all I've got.'

'In that case, talk to Pete Wilson's sister. I'll give you the address. The word is young Gary left her in the family way. She might be brassed off enough to talk to you.'

'Thanks a lot,' Bernie said, standing up to go. 'You've been a big help as usual.' He counted out some money and gave it to Davey who put it in his dressing-gown pocket without counting. It was an oddly dignified gesture for someone who looked so decrepit.

'It was good to see you, Davey,' Bernie said, rather sadly. 'I won't leave it so long another time.'

Anna was still trying to make something useful of the bedspring. She had torn the tail off her shirt to make a pad to cover the leg of the bed so that the noise of banging didn't travel too far. Verity sat crosslegged on the floor, not helping, not hindering. Hers would normally be a placid face with nothing much written on it: a full-cheeked child's face, pleasant, willing, and responsive. She had recovered enough to eat cold fish and chips, but that had been hours ago and she was still morose and fearful, jumping at imagined sounds. Someone, Anna thought, had a lot to answer for.

'Tell me about your family,' Anna said. She had avoided the subject until now, thinking it might upset her. But every other attempt to cheer her up had fallen flat.

'What about them?' Verity said dully. 'Dad has an antique shop. And Mum, well, she's just Mum. She helps him sometimes when he's busy.'

'There must be something special about them. These idiots didn't mistake you for Princess Margaret. It's got to be something like money, or grudge.'

'I've been trying to think about that. Dad isn't a millionaire, if that's what you mean. He worries about the business, actually, and tells me off when I leave lights on. I don't think he could pay a ransom.' The thought seemed to make her desolate.

'Then probably they don't want money, so don't worry. Can you think of anything else? Has anything unusual happened lately?'

'I don't think so, not lately. There was an accident a few months ago, and the police came round. Mum and Dad were awfully upset about that. But it was ages ago.'

'Were they hurt?'

'It wasn't their accident. Someone was knocked down

in front of Dad's shop and Dad saw it happen. He had to identify the car, and it was awful because the man who got knocked over died.'

'But besides that, nothing's happened? They haven't won the pools or anything.'

'They don't do the pools. And they haven't told me about anything special.'

'Enemies? Business competitors?'

'I don't think so. Honestly, they don't talk to me about anything important.'

'Oh well,' Anna said, 'never mind. It wouldn't help us much anyway.' She left the bed-spring on the floor and sat on the bed. Her fingers were sore and she had a wicked headache. The back of her head was still spongy to the touch and throughout the afternoon she had suffered more short spells of nausea and faintness.

'What about you?' Verity asked.

'Me?' Anna said, surprised because so far Verity had shown very little curiosity about her. The conversations, such as they were, had been rather one-sided with Anna drawing Verity out.

'Well, I was just thinking about Mum and Dad. They'll be out of their minds with worry, won't they? And I wondered who's going to worry about you?'

'I'm hoping no one's been told,' Anna said, not very hopefully. 'Because it's no use worrying if there's nothing to be done. Just a lot of aggravation and pain for no result.'

'But suppose they put our pictures in the papers or on telly? They often do when people get kidnapped.' This thought encouraged Verity as nothing else had. She even smiled.

'In that case,' Anna said, smiling too, 'I hope it's a bloody good picture.'

'I've always wanted to be on telly,' Verity said dreamily. 'Haven't you?'

*

'It was good of you both to come in,' Mr Brierly said, as if Bernie and Johnny weren't in his office at his request. 'Perhaps a little something to keep out the cold.' Gusts of rain rattled at the window. Daylight had died an early death. Brierly left the room to fill a jug with water.

'Bang goes any overtime we might be hanging on for,' Johnny said. 'We can't expect that *and* a lick at the office bottle.'

Bernie only grunted.

'Any luck?' Johnny asked. 'Or just sore feet like me?'

'It's Sunday,' Bernie said, shrugging his heavy shoulders.

Brierly returned with the jug. He unlocked a cupboard under the bookshelves and released the clients' bottle of VAT 69.

'Well, now,' he began, when everyone had settled with his watery drink. 'You may have been wondering why you haven't crossed paths with the official enquiry during the course of the day. I have managed to exchange a word or two with some old friends, and the answer is fairly simple. The police already know the reason for the abduction and have the situation well under control.

'It would appear that Verity Hewit's father Roland is due to appear for the prosecution in a case against Richard William Dutch for the murder of Reuben Irving. I believe that you, Mr Schiller, have already been given some indication that this is at the bottom of the muddle.'

'That's right,' Bernie said non-committally.

'The police are assuming that by holding Hewit's daughter, certain parties will be hoping to stifle or subvert Hewit's testimony. Presently, they are looking among Dutch's associates and are confident that they will uncover something soon.'

'What have they got?' Bernie asked.

'Nothing yet. But as I've said, they are confident they are looking in the right place.'

'Are we wasting our time, then?' Johnny said.

'I'm afraid it might seem so.' Brierly lapped delicately at his glass.

'What worries me,' Bernie said thoughtfully, 'is that this whole thing smacks of amateurism. And the thinking behind the pull is unrealistic. The people who associate with Willy Dutch are pros. I can't see them thinking they could turn a police witness. At the beginning, yes, but not after all this time.'

'That aspect has been taken into consideration,' Brierly murmured, 'but the consensus of opinion has veered towards the notion that without Dutch at the helm, his friends are disorganized and without direction.'

'And another thing,' Bernie said politely, 'is that the boys who did the pull were described as very young.'

'I don't think Henry Ames can be much over twenty,' Johnny agreed at last, 'and if he really was the finger-man, he certainly left himself out in the open longer than was sensible. A lot of people know his face now.'

A short silence followed, during which Brierly looked narrowly at both of them. Then he finished his drink and stood up. 'May I take it then that you wish to proceed along the lines you have drawn for yourselves?' He toyed with his empty glass. 'Well, thank you, gentlemen. I have to add, though, that we need results fairly soon.'

Bernie and Johnny walked out on to the wet High Street together. 'That was touch and go,' Johnny said. 'I thought he was going to suggest we continue on our own time, and at our own expense, if at all. The old bugger's going to have to get in a couple of stringers to cover for us, and he's crapping himself at the extra expense.'

Bernie looked up into the rain and dug his hands in his pockets. 'I hope they've got somewhere warm,' he said. 'It's a bit parky now.'

'Yeah, flaming bloody July,' Johnny said more soberly. 'Fancy a pint, mate? You're looking whacked yourself.'

'Not now, thanks. I thought I'd go and talk to the
Prices. Spread the glad tidings.'

'Don't they know yet?'

'I haven't said anything. I thought she might wangle
something, you see. But it's been over twenty-four hours
now. If she couldn't pull out at the beginning, there's not
much chance now.'

'One of those witnesses said she got bashed.' Johnny
turned his collar up and avoided Bernie's eyes. 'There's
still a chance. She's nobody's fool, you know.'

'I know,' Bernie said, moving off towards his car.
'Well, see you tomorrow.'

He drove to Anna's home, north of Holland Park
Avenue, and parked close to the house. Standing outside
with rain dripping lazily on to his bare head, he hesitated.
The Prices' curtains had already been closed against the
wet night. A cosy golden light showed through them, but,
further up, the windows glared blankly back at him. He
rang the bell, and Bea Price came to the door wearing a
Lea and Perrins plastic apron over her smart suit.

'Come in, Mr Schiller. You're wet through,' she said
warmly. 'We're just having a glass of wine before supper.'

He followed her in. Selwyn was typing by the window,
surrounded by balls of screwed-up paper like fallen
blossom after a strong wind. The television was on with
the sound turned down, and tiers of clean faces mouthed
a silent hymn into the room.

'Bernie!' Selwyn shouted happily. 'Just the man to share
a jar with. This measly drip of words wouldn't wet a
moth's tongue. Where's the gusher, I ask myself? You've
saved me from death by constipation.'

Bea put a glass in Bernie's hand and poured wine into
it. Selwyn came round behind his desk, looking thirsty.
'Feed me till I want no more,' he sang hopefully.

'That's bread of heaven, not wine of Algeria,' Bea said,
filling his glass. 'I don't know how you expect to write

poetry when you get things wrong like that.'

'I married a pedant,' Selwyn said, hugging her. 'She's the thorn in my flesh, the goad to my back and what's more, she can spell.'

'I can count, too,' Bea said tartly, 'and that's your fourth glass. How about leaving some for Mr Schiller.'

'Open another bottle, then. You're so sharp tonight, you shouldn't even need the corkscrew.'

'What I don't understand is why someone who talks as much as you do has such trouble writing,' Bea said in a voice like spiced honey. 'He's always complaining he can't find the words, Mr Schiller. But just listen to him. You won't hear the lack.'

This effectively silenced Selwyn long enough for Bernie to say, 'I'm afraid I've brought some bad news. Anna's missing.'

'Only 'cos she can't throw straight,' Selwyn crowed, slow to change gear. And then, 'Leo? What do you mean she's missing?'

'She was mixed up in a kidnapping yesterday afternoon, and got taken away with the other girl who was grabbed. She was having a go.'

'Oh, the fool!' Bea exclaimed. 'Why didn't someone stop her?'

'She was on her own at the time,' Bernie said sadly. 'I suppose she thought she could help. It was just a kid they were after, you see.'

'She couldn't just stand by,' Selwyn said, 'and no more would I.'

'Then you're a fool, too,' Bea said angrily. The thought frightened her.

'Listen, don't worry about it too much,' Bernie said awkwardly. 'The police are looking for her and we're looking for her so it won't be long before something turns up.'

'I'd better stop her milk then,' Bea said.

'Good God!' Selwyn exploded. 'Here am I, expecting sawn-off fingers in the post, and you want to stop the milk! Women!'

'That's not the way to look at it, Mr Price,' Bernie said quickly. 'That's all moonshine. Try and be calm and practical. You won't be able to help if you go off the deep end.'

'How can we help?' Bea asked.

'Well, if any message comes to this house, you can tell me straight away. Then there's Mr Kovacs, you'll have to let him know, or he'll be worried too.'

'Poor Gene,' Bea said, 'he'll be so upset.'

'Upset!' Selwyn repeated. 'He'll be cracking up, like I am.'

'And then, there's her mother and her sister,' Bernie ploughed on. 'One of them might ring here if they can't get an answer upstairs.'

'We'll tell them as little as possible,' Bea decided. 'Anna hates them fussing unnecessarily.'

'That's why I haven't told them so far. It's not as if they're a close family and it's kinder to leave it until there's some definite news.'

'Bea and I are more of a family than they are,' Selwyn said.

'I know, Mr Price,' Bernie said, 'that's why I'm here.'

CHAPTER 13

It was astonishing how cold it could be in a cellar room on an early July night, with rain blowing in through a broken window and gathering on a concrete floor. And how dark too. That at least gave the illusion of space. The walls hugged from four sides when you could see them, but darkness pushed them back out of sight.

Verity released herself from cold, fear, and hunger by
falling asleep, covered by the thin towel, her head on
Anna's lap. Anna stared into the black, wondering why
she bothered to keep her eyes open. But she didn't believe
the day was over yet. She thought Shake, Rattle, and Roll
would come back, and she didn't want to be caught
asleep, drowsy, or relaxed. It would be easy to be passive.
Cautiously, she touched the back of her head, digging
under the hair to wake the pain and remind herself of
everything she had to be angry about. More than the
brutality and neglect, it was the chilling indifference
which really frightened her. They wanted to be able to
ignore her and Verity: to be able to shut them up and
treat them with no more care than they would two
ladybirds in a match-box.

Her stomach was empty. She fed on uncertainty.

Presently she heard heavy boots on stone steps. She
touched Verity's shoulder, and said, 'Wake up, chicken.
The Goon Show's starting.'

She felt Verity stiffen and rub her eyes. The morbid
yellow light snapped on. Verity rolled away and jumped
up, shaking, on the other side of the bed. They heard the
sharp bark of bolts being drawn. Anna stood up too.
Born standing up and talking back, she thought
irrelevantly. It was a song for better times. Her hands
were trembling so she put them on her hips and forced
her chin up and shoulders back. There was a pause.

'They've lost the bloody key,' Anna said, feeling a
hysterical giggle rise in her chest. It wasn't funny. She
could hear Verity's teeth chattering. At last the key bit
into the lock and the thick door flew open, hitting the
wall with a bang. They stood there in the opening: four of
them this time. She would have to think up another
name.

'What the fuck you laughing at?' said the one she
hadn't seen before. He was a big man above the waist, but

he had jockey's legs.

'You, Lester,' she said, straightening her face. 'You look like the riot squad.'

'Think that's funny, huh?' he said, coming close to her. He had a harsh Glasgow accent. She could only see a reflection of herself in his shaded visor, stretched horizontally like in a fairground mirror. She stared into her own eyes and said, 'Not really. It's tragic, and so are you.'

'Who the fuck are you?' he demanded.

'Forget it,' she said. 'You wouldn't be interested.'

'Who is she?' he asked Verity. Verity seemed unable to speak. He beckoned Rattle. 'Ask her,' he said.

Rattle went around to Verity's side of the bed and leaned his hand against the wall above her head.

'You'd better tell us,' he said, his helmet very close to her face.

'Anna,' Verity said in a high scratchy voice.

'Anna what?' Lester said.

'Anna Lee,' Verity squawked.

'Where's she from? What's she up to?'

'I don't know. I promise I don't know.'

'Like fuck, you don't,' Rattle said, pressing his body against hers.

'Honestly, I'd tell you if I did.'

'She doesn't know a thing,' Anna said hurriedly. 'Leave her be.'

'You'd tell me if you knew?' Rattle said to Verity.

'Yes.'

'Because you like me, don't you?'

'Yes.'

'People who can't pull their weight always throw it around,' Anna said loudly. 'You must be really bored. You can't push people who already have their backs to the wall.' She had everyone's attention now. Rattle moved away from Verity, leaving her to shiver. 'And while I'm on the subject,' she went on harshly, 'how come I have to spout the Geneva Convention? Don't you know how to run a proper snatch?'

'I brought what you asked for,' Roll said.

'Thank you,' Anna said. 'Now why don't you all sling your collective hooks. Mass meetings in small rooms are a pain in the gluteus.'

'Want fucking jam on it, don't you?' Lester said.

'Jam on what? This is hardly the Ritz. You should sort something out between yourselves. I mean, is this the punishment wing, and if so, what for? Or is it business? In which case it wouldn't hurt you to stop trying to intimidate us and start treating us properly.'

'Fucking full of yourself, aren't you?' Shake said. 'You know why *you're* here.'

'Ah, the one who lost his helmet and then his head.'

'See! I told you the cow saw me,' Shake said to Lester.

'You must be kidding. I wouldn't have recognized my own mother in that bundle.'

'Says you,' Lester sneered.

'Think what you like,' Anna said indifferently, 'but I bet none of you would have known *me* again from one encounter.'

'Well, we're fucking stuck with you now,' Lester said, 'and if you want to stay out of hospital you'll fucking behave till the end of the match.'

'When will that be?'

'You're a nosey cow and no one has to tell you nothing,' Lester said angrily.

'Well, I don't want to embarrass you more than I have to,' Anna said sedately, 'but, if you haven't concluded your business by tomorrow, will someone bring me a packet of Tampax?'

'Oh, shit a brick,' Shake said and seemed to speak for them all. 'Women are nothing but a bloody nuisance.'

The room emptied soon afterwards. No one wanted to

stay and chat. 'Squeamish, aren't they?' Anna said with her ear to the keyhole. She heard the key turn in the lock, but only the top bolt shot home. They had left a clean slop bucket, fresh water, a couple of blankets, a roll of toilet-paper and another packet of fish and chips. The light went out; they would have to eat in the dark.

Anna's hands were still shaking and her heart was knocking so hard and fast against her lungs that it made regular breathing awkward.

She felt around for the blankets and the food and said, 'Let's eat, and then turn in. I'm knackered.'

Verity didn't respond.

Anna tried again, 'You're missing the midnight feast.' She put a chip in her mouth. It was cold, unsalted, and had absorbed a lot of grease in its short life. She swallowed it anyway, thinking that she'd better give all the adrenalin and supercharged metabolism something to work on or she'd never be able to sleep.

'You don't care, do you?' Verity said at length. 'You're just rude to them and shout and get their backs up. You don't care what happens to me.'

'Nothing's happened to you so far,' Anna said quietly, 'and the noisier I am, the less notice they take of you.'

'That's what you say,' Verity said, coming closer. She raised her voice, suddenly forceful. 'But you're just making trouble. You're making them lose their temper. And it's me they'll take it out on in the end.'

'No they won't,' Anna said. 'Come on and have something to eat. You'll feel better in a minute.'

'That's what grown-ups always say,' Verity said bitterly, 'but eating won't change anything. You're making things far worse than they are already, and you won't admit it. You just want to distract me.'

'OK.' Anna wearily pushed the food away. 'Forget it.'

Perversely, Verity sat down and began to eat. She ate voraciously. Then she screwed up the paper and tossed it on the floor.

'There!' she said. 'Am I feeling better?'

'Not if you don't want to,' Anna said. 'Listen, I know you're a well-brought-up girl, and you probably do what you're told at school too, but there are times when you've got to make trouble. It may be hard for you to believe, but some people don't deserve respect or good manners. And there are times when being polite and passive and timid only gets your rear-end kicked.'

'That's what you say,' Verity said. The bed shook as she lay down. 'But I think you're just getting me into trouble and I don't think you mind what I feel at all.'

'Of course I mind,' Anna began.

'That's not true,' Verity said. 'Grown-ups always say they mind, because they're supposed to, aren't they? But they don't really. When it comes down to it, they do just what they want to, and then they say they did it because it's good for us.'

'OK,' Anna said, suddenly feeling deflated and guilty, 'I know what you're talking about, and you're probably right.'

'That makes a change,' Verity said, and started to cry uncontrollably. Her whole body shuddered as if she were freezing. Anna unfolded the two blankets and tucked them around her. Then she stood under the window breathing in the damp night air and tried to clear her mind.

'Please don't leave me alone,' Verity said in a voice choked with crying and muffled with blankets.

'I'm not going anywhere,' Anna said, turning back to the bed.

'I'm sorry, really. I didn't mean it, honestly.'

'Don't worry about it.' Anna yawned.

It was cold and she got in under the blankets. Verity curled up close to her.

Anna said, 'Try trusting me a bit. You seem to trust

them more than you trust me. You shouldn't, you know. They may be holding all the cards, but that doesn't mean they know what they're doing. They're very young for this sort of racket and not bright enough.'

'But it isn't safe to talk back and cheek them,' Verity mumbled, her voice clogged with tiredness.

'It might be even more dangerous to let them walk all over us. They've got too much of an edge already. We can't let them take more.' Her words had the lonely sound they get when no one is listening. Verity had fallen suddenly and soundly asleep. Anna rearranged the blankets so that they covered her completely. On the corner of one of them she felt a sharp fibrous piece of stapled paper. She ran her fingernails under the ends of the staple, straightened it and drew it out of the blanket. The paper was tiny, no more than twice the length of the staple. She slid it carefully into one of the long side pockets of her denims.

She lay in the dark, listening to the wind and the rain as it spattered against the window and dripped through the hole on to the floor. Verity breathed evenly and quietly with nothing more than a tiny rasp as she inhaled. Cautiously, Anna turned on her side and felt under the mattress until her hand encountered the hammered bedspring. She eased herself off the bed and with the spring in her hand padded over to the door.

During the day, she had managed to straighten about three inches of the steel and re-bend the end of it into a crude L. She fitted it into the keyhole. It travelled through to the other side, which meant that the key had not been left in the lock. She withdrew it until just the L was left inside and fished around, twisting and turning it in search of the tumbler. After several minutes of fruitless probing, she sat back on her heels and thought about it. There did not seem to be a tumbler there at all. It was an old door, so presumably it would be an old lock. She tried to remember what the innards of old locks looked like. A diagram of a cylinder lock sprang readily into her mind as irrelevant images often do. She rubbed her eyes to banish it. The course she had once attended on theft prevention was too long ago and at the time it had just seemed like Chubb advertising anyway. She knelt forward again and this time inserted the wire at a steep upward angle. It travelled about two inches before it met resistance. She pushed and the wire slipped over whatever was holding it with a jolt. She drew the wire down again, angling it differently and pushed again. Same result. After seven more attempts she managed to push the resistance up. She took the wire out of the keyhole and sat crosslegged on the floor and thought about it some more.

Obviously it was a simple spring and bolt lock. This was easier, because nothing had to fit perfectly. If you could hold the spring up with one piece of wire, then you should be able to tickle the bolt back with another. She felt along to where the door met the jamb. But the door fitted tightly and there wasn't enough space to get at the bolt from there. She would have to find it inside the lock itself. And that meant she had to straighten yet another three inches of wire.

She massaged some warmth into her cramped fingers and went back to bed.

CHAPTER 14

In such deprived circumstances, Anna thought, happiness would be clean underwear and a bar of soap, those small things she never thought about at the beginning of a normal day: clean sheets, having a wash or a shower as the mood took her, cleaning her teeth if she remembered, putting on clean clothes, brushing her hair.

Anna ran her fingers through hair that needed a wash and hadn't been brushed for two days. Her scalp itched. Verity's comb was no substitute for a good stiff brush.

She undressed and wiped herself over with the damp towel. It was quite grubby by now, but it was more important to keep the bucket of water clean for drinking. She shook out her stale smelling clothes and put them on again. Breakfast was water drunk from cupped hands.

Verity still lay in bed with the grey blankets cuddled up under her chin. She had not stirred when Anna got up, and Anna was not sure whether she was asleep or just playing possum. She didn't know, either, if she should rouse her or leave her, so she roamed around the prison counting paces and bricks and trying to estimate the position of a sun she couldn't see. Six paces from the wall to the window, and five paces from the door to the wall; a small domain, high walls dwarfing the floor. Anna could imagine they had crept inwards during the night. Walls playing grandmother's footsteps. Close your eyes and they slyly inch towards you. A disturbing fantasy; Anna shook her head to discourage it and jarred the dull headache into feeble life. The swelling on the back of her head was going down and the broken skin had crusted over, but she thought uneasily about boxers and divers and lost brain cells.

Depression was taking hold fast: she could feel her willpower withering like an unused muscle, and faced with another full day of nothing but a series of minute and pointless activities, she was drawn towards sleep. She could lie down, close her eyes and let the hours fade away by themselves.

Instead, she stood upright, feet apart, and began to swing her arms in circles, whirling them up past her ears and down till they brushed her thighs. Twenty of those. Then twisting her torso as far as it would go, left and then right. Then down to touch the toes, and then knee bends.

Twenty of everything.

'What are you doing?' Verity said, sitting up.

'Waking up,' Anna puffed.

'We do that at school,' Verity said. 'It's silly.'

'Well, at least I'm getting warm.' She did twenty high kicks to stretch the muscles in her legs.

'Can you do handstands?' Verity asked, getting interested. Anna stood on her hands. Her head protested.

'Can you?' she asked in return. Verity scrambled off the bed and showed her. Then she did two walk-overs. One in each direction. There wasn't enough space for more.

'Great,' Anna said in approval.

'I used to go to the Gym Club,' Verity said, 'but I'm too old now. It's for kids, really.' But she put a folded blanket on the floor and amused herself by standing on her head for a while.

Anna retrieved the mutilated bed-spring from under the mattress, and sitting crosslegged on the floor began the long painful business of straightening the coils at the other end. In front of her, a woodlouse, like a tiny armadillo, trundled purposefully across the floor, circum-navigating the broken glass. When it reached the wall under the window, it climbed vertically upwards for eighteen inches. Then, losing hold, it fell and lay curled in a ball on the floor. After a few seconds, it straightened out, turned around and started back in the direction it had come from. It didn't seem at all discouraged by its failures or by the stupidity of its efforts. Born only to persist, Anna thought. It set a good example.

He was a man of about forty-five with stooped shoulders and thinning dun-coloured hair. Prominently displayed on his white coat was a round Union Jack badge with 'Made in England' written on it in bold gothic lettering.

Johnny paid for his tea with a five-pound note and left the change on the counter while he drank. The van smelled of stale onions. Overhead, late commuter trains rolled heavily into Charing Cross. It was nine-thirty, Monday morning.

'How's business?' Johnny asked amiably.

The man sniffed. 'People still got to eat and drink,' he said thinly.

'If they can,' Johnny said. 'Must be all right for tourists here.'

'Foreigners always got money,' the man said critically. 'It's us suckers born and bred here who have to scrape a living.'

'It's not getting easier.' Johnny nodded.

'We used to rule the world. Now look at us.' He sniffed again.

'Army?' Johnny asked.

'Cyprus in '59,' the man said, straightening up. 'Country's gone soft, no leadership. Yourself?'

'Signals,' Johnny said. 'I came out five years ago. Should've stopped in if you ask me.'

'You ought to come to one of our meetings,' the man said, tapping his badge with a greasy thumb. 'We could do with a few more who know what's what.'

'As a matter of fact, I was talking to a feller the other day. In there—' Johnny nodded towards the arcade— 'and he was saying something similar. Henry Ames. D'you know him?'

'Oh, him.' The man curled his upper lip. 'These young berks are just in it for the badges and the chance to duff someone over. Mind you, we need the ranks swelled, so I'm not knocking them.'

'Pity. I thought he was more serious than most. Fact is, I'm looking for him. I lent him some of my tapes, see, and I want them back.'

'You'll be lucky. Another soft scrounger, that one is. What sort of tape was it then?'

'Some of Churchill's speeches,' Johnny said, hoping

fervently he wasn't way over the top. 'I played them at a youth group round Victoria way, but the little bastards didn't want to know.'

'They wouldn't, would they,' the man said contemptuously, 'not unless he played a guitar and picked his nose in public. Pearls before swine, I call it.'

'Well, Henry seemed interested,' Johnny persevered.

'You must have quite a sales patter to get that little sod interested in anything,' the man said, eyeing Johnny curiously. 'You know, you really ought to come to a meeting. We need persuaders. Someone to spread the word. You could play your tapes, preach to the converted for a change.'

'Not unless I get them back, I can't,' Johnny said gloomily. 'You don't know where I could find him, do you? I thought he hung around here.'

'Haven't seen him for days. He lives off the Black Prince Road, though, same as me. I could give you the address, if you like,' the man said, looking meaningfully at the money on the counter.

Johnny reluctantly pushed it towards him. 'For the cause,' he said. 'You don't often meet a patriot these days.'

The man reached behind the counter and brought out a garish yellow and black pamphlet headed 'Made in England'. 'That's us,' he said, licking a stub of pencil. He wrote laboriously on the back of the paper and gave it to Johnny. 'There's a meeting Friday. Maybe I'll see you.'

'I wouldn't be surprised,' Johnny said, putting the paper in his pocket. 'I shouldn't mind meeting a few I could see eye to eye with.'

The lift was out of order. Bernie slowly climbed the concrete mountain of stairs to the seventh floor and out on to the corridor that served the flats on the north side of the block. About halfway along he saw a woman in a tidy grey suit leaning with both elbows on the edge of the balcony. She was breathing heavily. Yvonne Wilson's door was just behind her. Bernie rang the bell.

'No one in,' the woman gasped. Bernie leant beside her and joined in the heavy breathing.

'Nice view,' Bernie said, when he could. They could see the Oval looking like half an avocado pear resting on a generous slice of South London. 'Are you looking for Yvonne Wilson, too?'

'Yes,' she said and added, 'Social Security.' The wind caught her hair and stood it on end. Behind them a short black woman, as broad as she was long, walked past carrying two loaded carrier bags which hardly cleared the ground.

'Do you know where Yvonne Wilson is?' Bernie asked her.

'Gone,' she said, trudging on, rolling like a sailor from the effort, drops of sweat oozing from her lip and forehead.

'Gone where?'

'Brighton.'

'How long for?'

The woman finally stopped, putting her bags down where they spilled baked beans and cat food around her feet. 'Got to use my breath for breathing,' she said at last. 'That damn lift.' Presently she recovered enough wind to add, 'Get a pair of wings and come back tonight, man. Yvonne be back then.'

Bernie and the social worker helped her collect her wayward tins and she toiled wordlessly away.

'At least now we have gravity on our side,' the woman said, as she and Bernie went slowly down the stairs. The local graffiti told them what to do with Arsenal, Millwall, and Lambeth Borough Council and informed them that Gladys and Sue loved Mick. Further down, Maggy also loved Mick.

'Popular bloke, Mick,' Bernie remarked. Later on another message told them what Greg had done to Lynne, and what Mac was going to do to Greg if he had half a chance. Maybe he had already done it, or maybe Greg had seen the writing on the wall and moved somewhere else. Nor was religion neglected. Near the third-floor fire door someone had sprayed 'Jesus Saves' and someone else had added 'Green Shield Stamps.' But mostly writers stuck to the few words everyone can spell without being taught in school.

They emerged into broken sunlight. High above them patches of cloud passed uncertainly across the sun, promising both rain and shine, and making the tower of human cages look tawdry and insignificant.

'We deserve a cup of tea,' Bernie suggested.

'Don't we?' the woman agreed. 'There's a place over there.' She pointed across the car park and the main road to a row of small shops that had somehow survived redevelopment.

It was a small place, nearly clean, with a huge student's painting of the Acropolis on one wall. Two urns steamed fitfully behind a plastic display case full of shrivelled doughnuts, Lyons apple pies, and Penguin biscuits. A fat boy roused himself sufficiently to pour two cups of tea before subsiding again over his stained copy of *Spider Man*.

'My name's Nancy,' the woman said, putting her brief-case on the chair beside her and trying to rearrange her windblown hair. Bernie introduced himself too, and for a moment they sat quietly sipping their tea.

'Honestly, it makes me sick,' Nancy said suddenly, putting her cup down with a jolt that slopped tea into the saucer. 'She made the appointment herself, filled in the card and everything. You'd think the least she could do was be there.'

There was grey in her hair and worry lines between her

brows, but her eyes showed the innocence of good intentions.

'No, I shouldn't say that,' she went on, collecting herself. 'Yvonne has her problems. But I do wish she'd show a little more willingness to solve them.' She mopped the puddle in her saucer with a piece of Kleenex and put it neatly in the dented tin ashtray in front of her. More than half her anxiety seemed to be caused by keeping her own outraged emotions in check.

'I don't know the family,' Bernie said, watching her sympathetically. 'I'm looking for the brother, myself.'

'Peter?' she said, 'Oh, you must be his Probation Officer. Well, I wouldn't expect to find him at Yvonne's, if I were you. It's such a mess, that family.'

'Since Yvonne got into trouble?' Bernie asked.

'Oh, long before then.' Nancy tapped her head as if it contained the family archives. 'Everything from supervision orders when they were in Primary School. But I only got involved after the father left, and the mother and Yvonne were rehoused.' She gestured with her thumb at the building they had come from. 'Peter went to live with the father and his new wife so I didn't see much of him till he got out of hospital and moved in with the mother and Yvonne.'

'Hospital?' Bernie said confusedly. 'No one told me that.'

'I wonder why not,' Nancy said. 'I'd've thought it was crucial. They say he's slightly brain-damaged now. He nearly killed himself sniffing aerosol cans of painkiller. That's why he acts a little sub-normal now. Not that he's a bad sort really. It's more the fault of the company he keeps. In fact, you could say that of Yvonne and the mother too. They weren't doing too badly till the mother went off with that man from the railways and left Yvonne to look after Peter. Then his friend moved in and there was all that trouble about cohabitation when Yvonne lost her benefit.'

'Gary Natt?' Bernie asked.

'Oh, you know him too?' Nancy said, twisting her wedding-ring round and round. 'Well, I'm not surprised. You know what I mean by bad company then. Anyway, we no sooner got that mess sorted out when Yvonne says she's pregnant. You know—' she looked round guiltily—'I sometimes wish girls like that would have their tubes tied at birth. I know it sounds awful, but she'll never be able to cope with a baby. I shouldn't be talking like this, but sometimes I get so discouraged.'

'It's Monday morning,' Bernie said with a smile. 'We all feel like that sometime or other.'

'It's just that some families seem doomed from the start.' She rested her chin on her clenched fist. 'You know, my husband is a physicist and he comes home in the evening complaining about his assistants. They're wearing him out, he says. They've all got degrees and about five A-levels apiece and I don't know what he's talking about. Life's not fair, is it?'

'You mustn't lose faith,' Bernie said. 'People need a lot of help, whoever they are.'

'You're right. And it's not Yvonne's fault she's so incompetent. Or rather, it's only partly her fault. I mean the help's there. The opportunities are there. But she isn't clever enough to make use of them.'

'Speaking of which,' Bernie said, 'it's getting urgent that I have a word with Peter, or he'll be in a grand old mess too.'

'Oh dear.' She was twisting her wedding-ring furiously now. 'Has he missed an appointment too? I often think it's incompetence more than anything that gets them into trouble. Well, I can give you the mother's address if you haven't got it already, but I don't suppose it'll be much help.'

Out of her briefcase came a depressingly thick folder, and reading over Nancy's shoulder, Bernie jotted down

Pete's mother's address. He also memorized the father's which was typed beneath, but, like Nancy, he didn't really believe it would be much use.

'I do wish our departments would co-ordinate a little more closely,' she sighed. 'I'm always finding I haven't been given sufficient information.'

'You've been very kind,' Bernie said as they prepared to leave. Nancy straightened her jacket and picked up her case. She said, 'Actually, it's done me good to chat to you. The people in the office are so young now, and they really think there's something they can do. I've been at this job for fifteen years now, and I'm getting tired.'

'I know what you mean,' Bernie said, shaking her outstretched hand. 'Well, good luck anyway.'

'You too,' Nancy said, and moved away across the pavement, her grey skirt swinging against her thin calves. She did look tired, Bernie thought. And since it was Monday morning, he wondered how she would look by Friday night.

He spent the next twenty minutes looking for a working telephone. When he found one, he rang the office. Beryl said, 'The Commander's on the other line, but I'm glad you called. I've got one or two messages for you.'

'That's all right,' Bernie said, 'it was you I wanted anyway. Listen, can you get in touch with your admirer at Criminal Records and see if you can come up with something on Pete Wilson, Gary Natt, Jack Hardaker, and Eric Tozer? It's names of Probation Officers I'm after. I don't think current addresses are going to be much good. I've got a couple I'm going to try, but I'm not betting on them.'

There was a pause while Beryl wrote down the names. Then she said coyly, 'I'll see what I can do. It's not a source I can push too hard, but I'll do my best.'

'I'd be very grateful,' Bernie said, grimacing to himself and scratching his head.

'Well, since it's for you, Mr Schiller,' Beryl simpered. 'This is a terrible to-do, isn't it? We're ever so disorganized here.'

'Not you, Beryl,' Bernie said cajolingly. 'Now, what about those messages?'

'First,' Beryl said, quickly becoming efficient, 'Mr Crocker called. He's watching a house near Black Prince Road, and he wants a meeting. Then, there's a Mrs Bessy Corde. She wants to see you too, but not at her place, she says. She's doing some shopping at Peter Jones this morning, and if you can arrange to be choosing a suitcase there at about eleven o'clock, she'll pick you up.'

Bernie looked at his watch. He said, 'I can just about manage that. I take it Johnny will be ringing in again?'

'Yes, in about three-quarters of an hour. What shall I tell him?'

'Let's see,' Bernie said thoughtfully. 'The Green Dragon. That's a pub near Vauxhall Bridge, not far from where he is now. Say, twelve-thirty.'

'I'll tell him,' Beryl said. 'Oh, it's all such a muddle. By the way, a Chinaman's rung up twice already this morning. He keeps saying that Miss Lee's got his car or something. I can't understand a word he says.'

'That's Mr Minh, I expect,' Bernie said. 'He's not Chinese but I'll ring him later. Anything else?'

'Not at the moment.' Beryl sneezed, and Bernie could hear her fumbling for a tissue and blowing her nose. Then she said, 'It's so awful, all this, Mr Schiller. I was up half the night ringing round for replacements, and now I'm working with complete strangers. My routine's totally disrupted. And then Mr Maitland rang in this morning to say he's in bed with gastro-enteritis. He's usually so reliable and now I have to find a replacement for him too.'

'Phil's sick?' Bernie said thoughtfully. 'That's too bad.

Well, it's a good thing you're so efficient in an emergency.'

'I've got to be,' Beryl sniffed, 'with you lot gadding about. The Commander needs someone he can rely on.'

CHAPTER 15

Bernie avoided the scented mayhem of the ground floor at Peter Jones by walking up the wide staircase from the King's Road side. He pushed through the swing-doors and found himself surrounded by handbags and well-dressed women. Feeling extremely conspicuous, he threaded his way through to the comparative neutrality of luggage.

'Hello, dear,' Bessy said. 'You look like a bull in a china shop, if you don't mind me saying.'

'You're a sight for sore eyes yourself,' Bernie replied in ill-concealed wonder. She was covered from top to bottom in turquoise linen with flamboyant appendages of chiffon and ostrich feathers sprouting from head, neck and cuffs.

'Me Tatler togs,' she said with a giggle. 'The brewery's having a posh do today, and besides, you never know when you'll get run over, do you? If I've got to go, I'd rather go gorgeous.'

'No other way, for you,' Bernie said.

'Thanks, dearie,' she said seriously. 'Now, what we were talking about yesterday—there's a bit of a scream on and I've had visitors round. I thought you'd like to know.'

'That's right,' Bernie said, 'I would.'

'Only first—' she looked him straight in the eye—'there was something I wanted to ask you. About my sister's girl, Charmian.'

'I see,' Bernie said, looking straight back, 'go on.'

'Well, Charmian and her husband have this little restaurant near the power station, doing quite well, really. Only they'd be doing much better if they had a licence.'

'I see,' Bernie said again. 'What's the problem?'

'Well, Charmian's husband had a bit of trouble a while back. Not what he did, mind you. More what he didn't do. He wasn't in for whacks, just for drinks. But Old Bill doesn't always know the difference.'

'Big, was it?'

'Biggish,' Bessy said simply. 'Anyway, he doesn't mess about anymore, and that's a promise. But there's no forgive and forget where the law's concerned. And his application's been turned down.'

'What about Charmian?' Bernie asked. 'Has she tried to get the licence in her name?'

'That's what we figured, Mr Schiller,' Bessy said, 'only she doesn't want to burn her boats. If she got turned down on her husband's form, that'd be that, wouldn't it? So we thought, if someone put in a good word for her, there'd be a fair chance at least.'

'All right,' Bernie said. 'I've still got a few friends, but I can't promise, you know that.'

'Oh, I know, Mr Schiller,' Bessy said calmly, 'but it might make all the difference. Now, back to business.' She put her gloved hand on his arm and led him to the railing where they leaned and watched the crowd below them on the ground floor. 'Well, you remember yesterday when we was talking. We mentioned Willy Dutch. Last night, as I say, I had visitors. Two of Willy's friends. You've probably seen them around, the bald one, Curly, and his mate, Dunwoody.'

Bernie nodded, and she went on, 'Anyway they wanted to talk about the same subject as you. Now, soon after they arrived, in comes a couple of detectives. No trouble or anything, just a half of bitter apiece, but the eyes are peeled. And this is what's getting up Curly's nose. They've got the heat on them for Verity Hewit's snatch. Business is very quiet already because of Willy Dutch being where he is, and the boys could do without the extra pressure. It seems as if they've heard the murmur about Gary Natt too, so you aren't the only one looking for him. You haven't found him yet, have you?'

Bernie shook his head.

'Well, I told them,' Bessy said, 'Little Gary couldn't steal a hubcap without breaking his finger, but they seem to think he's showing off. You know, trying to move out of the junior league and make the first division look silly. They say, and I don't know if this is true or not, but they say that when Willy got in lumber, Gary was going round mouthing off some scheme for rubbing out Roly Hewit.'

'Oh Lord,' Bernie said. 'What did you tell them?'

'Not a thing,' Bessy said. 'What do I know? Anyway, Gary's mother used to be a friend of mine, so I'd rather you saw him first. Not that I care much what happens to the little bleeder, but you know how it is, there's been too much trouble already and it's not good for business.'

After a pause while they both considered the state of business, she said, 'Listen, stay south of the river. That's where his mum is, his sister, and his mates. That's where he went to school and that's where he's always knocked around. He'd never come up here if it weren't for Willy and his brother.'

'Yes,' Bernie said, 'I'm off down there now.'

Anna nursed a split nail and a bleeding thumb. The spring had slipped from its improvised vice, catching her under the thumbnail. She examined her morning's work and thought she now had enough straightened steel to pick the lock. She hid the spring under the mattress again and sat sucking her thumb.

'Am I getting blackheads?' Verity asked, anxiously

fingering her nose.

'Not yet,' Anna said, looking closely. 'I'm more worried about my teeth. They seem to be growing mould. And my mouth feels like the bottom of a birdcage.'

'Maybe they'll bring us some soap and toothpaste,' Verity said.

'And an apple,' Anna said wistfully.

'Chocolate,' Verity sighed.

'Not without the toothpaste,' Anna said firmly.

'I'm so hungry, I could eat anything at all.'

'Well, don't look at me like that,' Anna said with a smile. 'Cannibalism is bad for the complexion.'

Verity giggled, and Anna was pleased. It was the first sign Verity had shown of humour or spirit. All in all, though, there was not much to be pleased with. She measured herself against their prison and found herself a failure: she was too big to squirm between the window-bars, too small to knock down the door, too weak to smash a hole in the wall, and her voice wasn't loud enough to summon help. With patience, she could probably pick the lock, but that would be no use unless the bolts were left undone. She would just have to wait for someone to make a mistake. It seemed to Anna that she had already spent too much of her life waiting for other people to make mistakes she could capitalize on: so many reactions, so few actions.

To distract herself, she started to replay in her mind as much as she could remember of Tottenham winning the FA Cup.

'What are you smiling at?' Verity asked.

Bernie arrived at the Green Dragon a quarter of an hour late. Close by, old buildings had been half torn down and the new ones had been abandoned only half finished. Neither the demolition nor the construction had been completed. The area looked destitute, but the pub was crowded.

He looked around for Johnny and finally picked out his curly head at the other end of the room. Johnny was playing darts with Phil Maitland. Bernie grinned, and went to the bar to order a pint of light and bitter and a sandwich before making his way over to them.

'Mugs away,' Johnny said, handing the darts to Phil, unaware of Bernie's approach.

'Hello, sunshine,' Bernie said, tapping Phil on the shoulder. 'How's the guts?'

'Dreadful, squire,' Phil said cheerfully. 'Just dreadful. Kept me up all night.'

'It won't do, you know,' Bernie said, leading them over to a quieter corner. 'Beryl'll have one of her turns if she finds out.'

'Sod Beryl,' Johnny said, raising his glass as if he had just proposed a toast.

'United we stand,' Phil said, following suit, 'divided we're in schtuck.'

'Well, that's all right then,' Bernie said. 'So long as you know. Johnny's filled you in?' Phil nodded. 'OK. What about you, Johnny? Did you get Claire's friend?'

'I've got an address,' Johnny said, 'and I've checked. People called Ames do live there. But I haven't seen Henry yet. I thought you might want a natter first.'

'Good. If he's there, we want to box a bit clever. He may be all we've got.'

'No luck with Gary then?'

'Not yet,' Bernie said, 'but Beryl may be coming up with some Probation Officers later this afternoon. And there's a couple of addresses. You could try those, Phil, since you're here.'

'Right,' Phil said. 'Point me and pull my trigger.'

'What've you got in mind for Henry?' Johnny asked. 'Team-handed, is it?'

'I think so,' Bernie said. 'It's a bit tricky. We want to scratch him for what he's got. And only then wheel him in.'

'How's that?'

'Well, it seems now that there are three parties on the warpath. Us, the law, and Willy's lot. The law's only interested in Willy's lot. But the word on Gary's got about. Don't ask me how. But it means we might trip over Willy's people. So we've got to get enough info to interest the law, and at the same time not leave anything lying around for Willy's people to pick up. Also, we want to be quick. The longer this goes on, the less I like it.'

'So it's certain,' Phil said slowly, 'that we're pointing in the right direction, I mean.'

'No,' Bernie admitted, 'but it's getting more likely. I mean, I'm chuffed Henry Ames is a South London lad, but we've got to get the link between him and Gary or we're right where we started. On the other hand we know it can't be Willy's boys, or they wouldn't have the wind up like they do.'

'So it's H or bust,' Johnny said into his beer.

'So far,' Bernie answered, a little grimly.

'I should get on,' Phil suggested, 'but I need a rendezvous since I can't ring the office.'

CHAPTER 16

'I wish we had a radio,' Verity complained. 'It's so boring stuck down here with nothing to do.' She had stripped the wool overstitching from the edge of one of the blankets and was making cats' cradles. Every now and then she co-opted Anna to help with a complicated one. It was wonderful, Anna reflected, how quickly their predicament had been transformed, for Verity, from terrifying to merely tedious. Anna hoped she would be able to enjoy the boredom while it lasted. It would become terrifying again at the turn of a key.

'What would you be doing now?' Verity asked, 'if you weren't here, I mean.'

'Oh, working, I suppose,' Anna replied idly.

'What do you do?' Verity persisted, and Anna suddenly woke up to the danger of telling her. She could easily be bullied into betrayal, and those yobs would take a dim view of harbouring a detective.

'Research,' she said, in the end. 'You know, finding out things people haven't got time to find out for themselves.'

'Looking things up,' Verity supplied, not very interested. 'I can't say I'd want to spend my life in a library.'

'Don't you like reading?' Anna asked, both amused and a little dismayed at how easily Verity was put off.

'It's all right,' Verity said and concentrated again on her piece of wool, leaving Anna free to wonder what was going on in the world outside. For at times it did seem incredible that only two days ago she had been having perfectly normal conversations with Johnny in the van. She had been able to eat a sandwich when she was hungry and make a cup of tea when she fancied one.

'If I were on a desert island,' she mused aloud, 'the one luxury I'd want with me would be a decent cup of tea whenever I wanted one. You can cope with anything, given a good hot cup of tea.'

Verity looked at her incredulously. 'Where would you get a cup of tea on a desert island?' she said scornfully. Then, when she had thought about it for a bit, she added, 'What I'd like is a moped. You could whiz up and down the beach like crazy and there'd be no one to tell you to slow down or that you were making too much noise.'

Anna grinned and Verity went back to her cats'

cradles. The end of childhood, Anna thought, must come
when you stopped wanting toys and believing in miracles.
Then she thought of Johnny buying the earliest edition of
the evening paper and rushing off, with complete
confidence each time, to phone his bookie: Johnny with
his innocent pride in each new car he possessed. She
wondered what he was doing now: what everyone at
Brierly Security was doing. Had she become a case for
them? The thought was comforting, because sometimes
she had an odd feeling that a black crevasse had opened
up and swallowed her and Verity whole, leaving no trace
of their existence behind. The idea that her absence was
as abnormal to her friends as it was to her made their false
position here both more real and more bearable.

'Listen,' Verity said, dropping the wool on the floor.
'They're coming.'

This time the door opened quietly.

'Hello,' Roll said, almost timidly. 'I've brought your
dinner.' He was holding a Safeway carrier bag. Rattle
loomed behind him in the doorway, tall and wasted,
moving nervously from one foot to the other. Without
Shake and Lester, the two seemed more ridiculous than
alarming. Rattle was armed with a chair-leg, but it
looked more substantial than he did.

'Does your mum know what you do in your spare time?'
Anna asked conversationally.

'Shut up,' warned Rattle.

'Do what?' said Roll, kneeling down to unpack his
carrier bag. Verity stirred uneasily and looked
imploringly at Anna.

'I remembered the soap this time,' Roll said, producing
it triumphantly. 'It's not new,' he added apologetically.

'We want another bucket of water,' Anna said.
'Separate buckets for washing and drinking.'

'Where are we supposed to find bloody buckets?' Rattle
snapped.

'That's your problem,' Anna said.

'It doesn't matter,' Verity put in quickly.

'Yes, it does,' Anna said firmly. 'It's unhygienic to wash and drink out of the same bucket.'

'There's one in the boiler-room,' Roll said. He handed Anna the inevitable greasy packet. He had bitten his fingernails down to the quick and his hands looked like stubby paws. It's pathetic, Anna thought, to be stymied by people like this. Looking down on him where he crouched over the Safeway bag, she thought he looked like a small boy. His helmet made a big round shape where his head should be and his shirt had come away from his jeans exposing a few inches of fine pale skin. He rummaged some more and came up with a paper bag.

'Give that here!' Rattle shouted, coming over. 'You don't want to show them where they are, you silly berk!' He snatched the bag. It had the name and address of a chemist on it, but Anna wasn't close enough to read it. She looked at the open door and then back. Rattle tore the paper bag from a box of Tampax. Roll looked up from his position on the floor, confused. Anna took a couple of deep breaths and edged towards the door.

'Anna!' Verity cried out. Anna stopped. Alone, or with a willing partner, she could have been through the door in seconds. She could have slammed it shut and turned the key in less time than it took to say 'Bye bye, suckers.' But she couldn't do it and leave Verity on the same side as Rattle and Roll. And Verity was rooted to the spot on the other side of the bed. She forced herself to say 'OK' in a perfectly normal voice and take the steps that put her firmly back beside Verity. It was as if the opportunity had never arisen, but now she was rigid with unexploded energy and her breathing was as uneven as if she had already sprinted a hundred yards.

'What's up?' Roll said, turning round.

'It's OK,' Anna said again. 'She isn't feeling very well,

that's all.' She patted Verity's shoulder gently but her hand felt like a dead claw.

'She's not getting sick, is she?' Roll said worriedly. 'We need her for the tape-recording.'

'Shut up,' Rattle said, screwing up the chemist's bag and going back to the doorway. 'You'll give the sodding game away if you keep bleating on the way you do.'

'We can be a bit friendly, can't we?' Roll protested. He picked up the two buckets and left the room, offended.

When he came back, he brought a cracked enamel bowl with 3C written on it in black laundry-marker. He flourished it proudly and said, 'I knew I seen it somewhere.'

Anna said, 'Good,' and Verity whispered, 'Thank you very much.'

'We don't want to arse around here all day,' Rattle snorted, pushing Roll through the door.

'Nor do we,' Anna muttered as the key turned and the bolts slammed home.

'You were going to run away and leave me,' Verity accused violently when the footsteps had died away. 'You just don't care, do you?'

'There was a chance for both of us,' Anna said.

'We'd've been caught,' Verity cried.

'We could've shut the door on them. For once they were both inside,' Anna said. 'It was a chance that won't come again, and we blew it.'

'I'm glad,' Verity said, tears streaming down her pale cheeks. 'It just isn't safe. You're going to make them treat us far worse.'

'Than what?' Anna asked, her temper going. 'You're consenting! That's what you're doing.'

'What do you mean?'

'Look,' Anna exploded. 'You think they're supermen. They're not. They're bloody cretins. You think they're looking after us! What a laugh! You're getting used to something that's completely outrageous. You're accepting it! I give up.' She threw herself down on the bed and covered her eyes with her arm to block out the sight of Verity's miserable face.

'Now you're shouting at me,' Verity wept. 'You're worse than they are.'

Jesus Christ! Anna thought. That's the limit! But they were stuck with each other, and she knew she had been harsh, venting the rage she felt on someone who didn't really deserve it. Verity was just very young and very passive and it wasn't her fault. She remained where she was, hiding behind her elbow, trying to regain some control, and listened to Verity sobbing.

After a few minutes Verity sniffed and said, 'All right, then, I won't help with that tape-recording.' Anna sat up and smiled at her.

'I won't!' Verity asserted weakly. 'They can't make me.'

'Oh dear,' Anna sighed, 'now you're picking the wrong thing to get stroppy about.' She got up and gave Verity a brief hug. 'The recording will be a message to your parents. And it's the only way you've got of telling them you're alive and well.'

'So I should do it?' Verity asked, relieved.

'Yes,' Anna said, 'But when you're doing it, try to say "we". Then my friends'll know I'm all right too.'

'OK,' Verity said, cheering up. 'Perhaps we can find some way of putting in a secret message.'

'Perhaps,' Anna said, not wanting to disillusion her. Verity unwrapped the fish and chips. Anna wasn't very hungry anymore so Verity ate most of it. Afterwards, Verity lay down and went to sleep, so Anna turned her attention to the box of Tampax. Both Rattle and Roll had handled it. She stripped the wrapping off and with great care folded the cellophane into a couple of squares of lavatory paper and put it in her jeans pocket.

CHAPTER 17

'What's round the back?' Bernie asked. They were sitting in Johnny's yellow Cortina outside a row of red-brick terraced houses. Each house had a few steps up to the front door and a few down to a narrow basement area.

'Nice,' Johnny answered. 'The yard backs on to a school wall, about twenty foot high. No one's going to bunk out that way.'

'Mmm,' Bernie said. 'What about into the neighbours?'

'Could do,' Johnny said. 'We can't stop that.'

'No,' Bernie agreed, 'but you'd better watch the street.' He got slowly out of the car, walked up the steps and knocked. The door opened six inches on to a pale face and a dark hall.

'Hello, Henry,' Bernie said, sliding his foot to stop the door closing. 'Can we have a word?'

'Get knotted,' said Henry, slamming the door against Bernie's sturdy boot. Bernie leaned inwards almost casually, like an elephant resting against a tree; the door eased open again.

'Give it a rest, lad,' Bernie said. 'I just want a chat. It might save you a bit of trouble.'

'Trouble?' Henry grunted from the hall. He was still hopelessly trying to close the door. 'You're the only trouble I've got.'

'Conspiracy, kidnap, consorting with a minor?' Bernie murmured softly. The door crashed open under his weight and fleetingly he saw Henry pounding down the dark hall and disappearing into a doorway at the end of it. Bernie sighed and stayed where he was. He leaned against the door-jamb and lit a cigarette. After a few minutes he heard the basement door opening cautiously.

He melted backwards into the hall so that he wouldn't be seen from below. Henry tiptoed up the basement steps to the pavement. He was about a dozen paces away from the house when he saw Johnny and began to run. Johnny chased him past three lamp-posts, and caught him by the fourth.

'Don't be so shy, Henry,' Johnny said, gripping Henry's arm in one hand and the belt of his jeans in the other. He was nearly six feet tall and built like a dancer. His hair was as short as velvet and he had attractive blue eyes topped by straight eyebrows. Johnny pushed him and he walked reluctantly back to the Cortina.

'Too flat-footed to do your own dirty work?' Henry sneered at Bernie when they joined him.

'You can't expect me to chase you all around the houses,' Bernie protested. 'I'm far too long in the tooth for that.'

'You do all right,' Henry muttered sulkily. 'Who the fuck are you, anyway?'

'This is Mr Schiller,' Johnny told him, 'and I'm John Crocker and you're Henry Ames. *Now* can we talk?'

'Give me one good reason.'

'How about Curly Bates and his friend Dunwoody?' Bernie asked mildly. 'Know them?'

'No.'

'Well, they know you,' Johnny said, 'and they're looking for you. Trouble is, the people they find tend to get all donged up. Mr Schiller, on the other hand, is the easygoing type. Talking to him doesn't hurt at all. Count yourself lucky he found you first.'

'Let's get in the car, shall we?' Bernie suggested. 'It's going to rain in a minute.'

'Your rheumatism?' Henry said nastily. 'Some hope. Why do I always get caught in the middle?'

'Happened before, has it, sunshine?' Bernie said, getting into the Cortina and leaning back comfortably.

Johnny shepherded Henry in beside him, and sat himself by the door. Bernie gave Henry a cigarette and lit it for him.

'We know all about Claire Fourie and Verity Hewit,' he began conversationally, 'so why don't you tell us your side of it?'

'I knew it wouldn't work,' Henry said bitterly. 'They swore blind nothing'd come back on me but why should they be right about this when they're wrong about everything else?'

'Who are we talking about?' Bernie asked. 'Gary? Pete? Jack?'

'They're so bleeding stupid,' Henry said. 'Everything they do turns to shit. Me, I've got three CSEs, but what good does that do me? I even stayed an extra year at school. And then? Sweet FA. They're always trying to drag me down.'

'Looks like they managed this time,' Johnny said.

'I've got potential,' Henry claimed, not listening, 'but it's those patronizing bastards in Hampstead who've got all the opportunities. They think it's all a big giggle, they do. Allowing me to live in that scrubby cellar: thought they were doing me a favour, didn't they? Didn't even have a telly, cheap fuckers. Well, I showed them. Every time I got that little nympho in the kip, I felt I had the whole lot of them on the end of my—'

'That's enough,' Bernie interrupted. 'Claire's only fourteen and you could be in a lot of bother on that score too.'

Henry looked aghast. In the end he said, 'Nobody told me. Typical, that is. I get shat on from every direction.'

'It's about time you came clean then,' Bernie said, 'and maybe some of it won't stick. When did your friends first approach you about this kidnapping?'

'I didn't know it was kidnapping,' Henry protested. 'You've got to believe that. It was when a pal of theirs got done for murder. Some big-time villain they're always on about.'

'Willy Dutch,' Johnny said. 'Let's have some names for a change.'

'Well, I don't know him. And I don't want to. Me and Gary and Pete and Jack were in the same year at school. Gary wanted to take after his brother Morris who was always a flash bugger. But Gary didn't really have it upstairs. He was always on about the jobs he was going to pull, but he's so useless, he'd get his fingers caught in a cigarette machine. Anyway he and the others and a Scotch maniac called Eric came to see me about three months ago.'

'What happened?' Bernie asked.

'They give me fifty quid, and we went up north to Camden Town. We sat in the motor outside a poncey second-hand furniture shop for a couple of hours. And then we see two girls coming down the road, a big horsy one and Claire. And Gary points to Claire's friend and says, "Her daddy needs a bit of a fright," see, "so we want you to knock around after the girl and tell us what she does and where she goes." So I said, "Why me?" And he said, "Because we don't want to be seen." That's how it happened.'

'And you agreed?'

'Well, fifty quid's fifty quid, innit?' Henry said reasonably. 'And there was more to come, Gary said. Anyway, I had nothing else to do, did I? It seemed better than stopping indoors.'

'So, how come you got involved with Claire and not Verity?' Johnny asked.

'It was silly really. See, I'd found out which school Verity went to, and I told the others where it was and what time she was let out, and what bus she took and so on, but they didn't seem interested. Too public I expect. Well, come the end of term, things changed a bit. But she didn't go out much except for shopping with her mother or when Claire came round. Well, one day, it was raining and Claire turned up in the morning and I didn't see anything till after dinner. I was getting proper fed up, hanging about in doorways, getting wet. Then the two of them came out with suitcases and I followed them to Charing Cross. Verity bought a ticket, and I thought, blow this for a lark, I'm not leaving London for sodding fifty quid which was nearly all gone anyway. So I was standing there, watching the train go out and wondering what to do next when Claire walks straight into me. And she says, "Oh, sorry," like she's a duchess or something. And then she says, "Haven't I seen you somewhere before?" ' Henry's mimicry of the middle-class accent was venomous.

'Anyway, I was fed up, like I say, so I says, all poncey too, "Excuse me for living. It's your amazing beauty, see, I can't keep away." Or something like that. I never thought she'd take me seriously, though. Anyway, it seemed useful. She could tell me when Verity was coming back. She had some money too, so we went and played Space Invaders in the arcade. That's how it started. Squatting in that poky bloody flat was her idea too. It gave her a thrill to have me living right underneath. She hates her parents, she says. All their bourgeois values, she calls them. What a laugh. It doesn't stop her taking their bourgeois money, I notice. Still, I never let on. Not even to those phoney students. I'm a good mixer, me. Not like some. They'd've stuck out like sore thumbs.'

'That's all very well,' Bernie interjected. He was getting increasingly impatient with Henry's whining monologue. 'But where are they now?'

'Who?' Henry asked innocently.

'Verity and Anna,' Johnny snapped. 'Who do you think?'

'Who's Anna? I haven't seen anyone since that day at

the swimming pool.'

Bernie and Johnny looked across him at each other and then looked hopelessly away.

'What do you mean, you haven't seen anyone?' Johnny said angrily. 'What about your mates? You were in this together.'

'Yeah, what about me mates?' Henry said pathetically. 'They owe me my second whack, don't they? Well, they're not in any hurry coming across with it, are they? Typical.'

In spite of the spitting rain, Johnny opened the window. The car seemed bunged up with individual frustrations. He took a deep breath to prevent himself from shouting.

'Stop yammering on about yourself,' he shouted. 'Where the hell are they?'

Startled, and for the first time, frightened, Henry caved in on himself. He sank deeper in the car seat and folded himself away from Johnny. He said, 'I don't know, I swear, I wish I did.'

Johnny took another deep breath, this time to shout even louder, but Bernie forestalled him. 'All right, Johnny, all right,' he said smoothly. 'Let's get this back to the office and see what we can salvage.'

Phil Maitland had acquired all of his education and most of his experience in the Military Police. He believed in a direct approach. He thought Bernie was too sleepy and too circumspect to be effective, Johnny too flash, Anna a light-weight. But he, Phil, was a double-top, bullseye man; nothing fancy, what's right's right, and what's wrong deserves a big stick. Time served in Malaya, Cyprus, and Northern Ireland had taught him a thing or two about human nature, but it hadn't left him with much subtlety or patience.

The Wilsons lived on the first floor of an old house in

Peckham. Phil went up two at a time, and hammered on their door.

'You Mrs Wilson?' he asked when it opened.

'Yerse?' she said, touching the lipstick at the corner of her mouth with a little finger.

'Well, I'm looking for your boy, Pete,' he informed her.

'He's not my boy,' she said lowering her blue eyelids in disdain. 'I'm the second Mrs Wilson, you might say.' She had a face, he thought, like a wrung-out flannel. None of her features were quite where they ought to be. The make-up and the intellectual glasses didn't help matters either. They served to point to the asymmetry rather than disguise it. She was young, though: to Phil's reckoning, too young for Pete Wilson's father.

'You won't find him here,' she went on, laying great emphasis on her h's as if she had just learned how.

'Where would I find him?' Phil asked impatiently. He knew the type; always trying to better themselves, he thought, making life a misery for anyone around.

'Don't ask me. He prefers the company of those friends of his to a respectable home,' she said indifferently. 'I wouldn't know where that sort goes. But if you ask me, it's a mercy we don't have to put up with him much. Mr Wilson's beginning to agree with me too. There are better things in life than trying to keep Pete out of trouble.'

'Do you know where any of his friends live?' Phil said. He heard the door to the street open and close. She heard it too.

'No,' she said quickly. 'Now, if you don't mind, I'd rather not be seen talking to you on the landing.' She stepped back and shut the door in his face. Stuck-up little cow, he thought as he turned to go.

Two men were waiting for him at the head of the stairs. 'You know Mr Schiller?' one of them said. The landing window was behind them, so he couldn't see their faces properly.

'I might,' Phil said, startled. He hadn't heard them come up.

'You can give him a message for us,' the man said.

'I might,' Phil said again, thinking that these must be the Dutch boys.

'Let's get out of here,' the other one said. 'This place stinks of Harpic and stewed prunes.' They went downstairs and out on to the street. Phil followed.

'I'm Clive Bates,' the man said when they were all outside, 'and this is my associate, Mr Dunwoody.' They were both wearing business suits, in slightly different shades of grey.

'Phil Maitland,' Phil said.

'Pleased to meet you, Mr Maitland,' Mr Dunwoody said politely. 'You were enquiring after Pete Wilson, I understand.'

'I might have been,' Phil said.

'That's no concern of ours,' Clive Bates said, fitting a black felt hat on to his naked pink scalp. 'But we think it's about time we got round a table with Mr Schiller.'

'He's a bit busy at the moment,' Phil began, 'perhaps . . .'

'We believe in commencing negotiations at the top,' Bates said firmly. 'So, will you communicate our request to Mr Schiller?'

'All right,' Phil said. 'I'll tell him you asked.'

'Yes,' Dunwoody said. 'We have a little interest in a place in Battersea. The Laundry. He'll know where to find us.'

'I'll tell him,' Phil repeated.

'Any time, till four in the morning,' Bates said. 'I know he's a busy man, but tell him that negotiations at this point in time would be in both our interests.'

'Well, thank you, Mr Maitland,' Dunwoody added courteously. 'Can we give you a lift anywhere?'

'Er, no,' Phil said, still a little stunned. 'I'm parked

round the corner.'

'Then arryvidairchy,' Dunwoody said. And they both crossed the road and got into a Daimler Sovereign parked ostentatiously on the other side.

'And arryvi-bloody-dairchy to you too, mate,' Phil muttered as he walked away to his Escort. He was feeling upstaged.

CHAPTER 18

'The trouble with Claire is she never gets spots,' Verity grumbled, drawing the cross-piece of the gallows. They were playing Hangman, sitting opposite each other on the floor and scratching on the cement with pieces of glass. 'Her tights never go wrinkly,' she went on, 'and her zip never slips down.'

'Is there a B?' Anna asked.

'No,' Verity said, scratching in the rope. The floor was already inscribed with numerous grids for noughts and crosses and boxes. 'I mean, she's so sort of perfect she never sweats and she makes me feel like a big lump.'

'Well, you aren't,' Anna said, suspecting that Verity wasn't really talking about Claire at all. 'And everybody sweats. How about an R or have I said that already?'

'No and no.' Verity dangled a head from the rope. 'When there are a lot of people in the room everyone looks at her. Everyone listens to her too, even the grown-ups.'

'Is she bright?' Anna asked, considering the mystery word with half her attention. So far she had -A--E-IO-.

'I get better marks than her at school, but nobody listens to me.'

Anna thought this was probably irrelevant. It was just that pretty girls get a lot more attention than ordinary

ones. Claire was undoubtedly very beautiful but Anna,
who had watched her closely, wondered if she was any
more interesting than most girls her age. She thought not.
But she said nothing to Verity because she didn't want her
to know how familiar she was with her friend. In the end
she said, 'Don't worry, Claire's just grown up faster than
you.'

'That's what Mum says.' Verity looked oddly satisfied
and Anna felt as if she had fallen into a trap. 'C?' she
said, at random. Verity added a bloated body to the
hanging head.

'Mum says I'll catch up in a couple of years, but I can't
see that happening,' she mourned. Again Anna had the
impression that Verity was not too unhappy with this state
of affairs. She was inviting compliments or comfort by
making the comparisons between herself and Claire, and
she seemed to be accustomed to receiving them.

Anna felt manipulated but she couldn't refuse the
comfort. She said, 'It's better to have your best time
ahead of you than behind you. Don't wish for too much
too young. It spoils the future. People who have everything when they're young can only look back when they're
older. What about M?'

'Grown-ups are always talking about the future,' Verity
said almost smugly, adding an arm. 'But when does the
future begin? I want to be happy now.'

Anna looked at the half-formed face opposite her and
felt frustrated. She had nothing to offer but clichés.
Instead, she said, 'W? P? F? G?'

Verity drew another arm and two legs. 'You're
hanged,' she said happily, completing the stick figure.

'What was the word?'

'It was dandelion. I'm bored with this now,' Verity
said, and sat back waiting for Anna to make another
suggestion.

*

Bea was feeling extremely awkward. Gene was sitting in Selwyn's chair and Selwyn was roaming, homeless, around the room looking as if he were about to sit on Gene's knee every time he passed him. It was his own fault, she thought. Pure cowardice had made him disappear into the bathroom until she had broken the bad news to Gene. Besides, what was wrong with the sofa?

On the other hand, Gene did not have a proper British respect for other people's castles. He never said, 'May I sit here?' giving her the chance to shepherd him into a different chair. He just sat wherever it suited him. Nor had he asked for the glass of water he was drinking now. He had simply gone to the kitchen and helped himself. Not that there was anything wrong with that, but it left Selwyn feeling usurped and herself with nothing to do. She would like to have indulged in a little avoidance too, by making tea for him. But now he already had the water and she was forced to sit opposite him and watch Selwyn pace restlessly.

She was aware, too, that Selwyn had never quite taken to Gene. It was all right when Anna was there to bridge gaps, but on his own Gene was just someone with whom he had nothing in common. And worst of all, subtly and unreasonably, they both seemed to be blaming the other for what had happened to Anna.

'I just don't understand how this situation could have occurred,' Gene was saying, looking hard at Selwyn.

'You should have insisted she went sailing with you,' Selwyn responded. 'She doesn't get out of London enough.'

'I wish I had more confidence in your British police,' Gene countered, laying rather more stress on 'your' than was absolutely necessary.

'Better than the FBI, anyway,' Selwyn muttered, moving behind Gene and addressing the back of his neck.

'At least they get things done,' Gene said, giving Bea

the distinct impression that he knew no more about the
FBI than Selwyn did. 'I don't know about you,' Gene
added, 'but I can't stand sitting around on my tuchus
doing nothing.'

'What's to be done?' Selwyn asked, unreasonably, Bea
felt, as he had spent most of the day saying that they must
do something.

'Well, I don't know about you,' Gene repeated,
springing to his feet, 'but I'm for drumming up a little
action.' And without stopping to explain, he left. They
heard the front door slam and his car starting up.

'Damned Yank,' Selwyn said. Now that he had vacant
possession of his own chair, he chose to sit meekly next to
Bea on the sofa. 'I don't know what Anna sees in him.
He's nothing but a yahoo.'

'He's young, handsome, and energetic,' Bea said
wistfully.

'So am I, woman,' Selwyn asserted.

'He's also sober,' Bea said conclusively.

'You!' Lester said. 'You, Anna, what's your name. Get
over there in the corner and shut up.'

Anna went to the corner, leaving Verity alone by the
window.

'If there's one peep out of her, belt her,' he said to
Rattle.

'You!' Lester snapped at Roll. 'Close the bleeding door
and stay there.' He had blustered in like a lion, Anna
thought, but there was little hope that he'd go out like a
lamb.

Shake carried the cassette-recorder and both he and
Lester advanced on Verity. She backed away from it as if
it was an instrument of torture and sat down abruptly on
the bed.

'What's up?' Shake sneered. 'Don't you want to talk to
your darling daddy?'

'Cut the chat,' Lester said, his thick shoulder muscles bunched up aggressively under his leather jacket. 'Let's get on with it.'

'What do you want me to say?' Verity quavered in a scared little-girl voice.

'Doesn't know what to say to her own daddy,' Shake said.

Lester said, 'Tell him you're all right, you're being treated well, but he'd better do what we tell him or he won't fucking see his little girl again.'

In her corner, Anna folded her arms tightly across her chest and bit her tongue. Verity started to cry.

Lester said, 'Shut your snivelling and start now.'

Shake pressed a key on the machine. 'Daddy?' Verity whispered.

'Louder!' Lester barked.

'Daddy,' Verity started again.

'Just a minute,' Shake said, 'the sodding thing won't start.' He pressed the key again and then three times more, but it wouldn't stay down and the recorder gave off clicking noises.

'What's up with it?' Lester asked, his neck going purple with anger. 'Did you put the sodding batteries in?'

' 'Course I did, what do you think?' Shake said, jabbing viciously at the key. 'Fucking Nip machines.'

Anna grinned spitefully. Lester looked up and caught her doing it. 'You!' he shouted, marching across the room. A shard of glass caught in the thick crepe sole of one of his boots, giving his footsteps a dot-and-carry sound. This made him even angrier, and he stopped to pick the glass out of his boot. Then, from almost point-blank range he hurled it at Anna. She ducked and it hit the wall behind her. He grabbed a fistful of her hair and tugged it so fiercely that she fell down on her knees.

'Get up, you bitch,' he screamed. Anna got up and refolded her arms. She could see that he was almost berserk with rage. Little gouts of spittle dotted the inside of his visor. She said evenly, 'You've got the cassette in the wrong way round. Either turn it over or wind the tape back.'

Lester said, 'Pissing superior cow,' and aimed a ferocious kick at her leg. She moved quickly so that his boot only grazed her shin, but it hurt enough to make her dread what would have happened if it had landed squarely. She was very frightened.

'Give over,' Shake said from the other side of the room. He sounded frightened too. Roll giggled nervously. The little room was clotted with everyone's fear of Lester. Anna wondered if he lost control regularly.

Tentatively, Shake said, 'Pack it in, mate. We've got things to do.'

Gradually the tension eased. Lester turned rigidly away and went back to Shake and the recorder. Anna slowly let go of a breath she had been holding for nearly fifteen seconds.

Shake turned the cassette over with fingers that trembled. The machine worked this time.

'Daddy?' Verity began again in a voice that wobbled. 'I . . . I'm all right, really I am. But, please, Daddy, do what they tell you or I don't know what'll happen. I'm sorry . . . We . . . we're being treated well, but . . .' she faltered and burst into tears again. Shake stopped the tape and played it back.

'I like that,' Lester said. 'I like where she cries. That'll make him sit up, that will.'

In a few minutes Anna and Verity were left alone again and the damp silence was broken only by Verity's noisy grief. Anna crossed the floor, covered with the marks of the afternoon's childish games, and put her arms round her.

'It's OK now,' she said, rocking the sobbing girl. 'It's OK. You did fine. It'll all be over soon.'

'It won't,' Verity cried, burying her wet face in Anna's shoulder. 'He can't pay. I know he can't. They're going to kill us. I know they are.'

'You don't know anything of the sort,' Anna said, stroking Verity's back as if she were a frightened animal. 'Your father has a house and a shop. He can raise money, if it's money they're after. You'll see. Everything'll be all right soon.'

'Will it?'

'Of course,' Anna said sturdily, hating herself and the role of false comforter. It was forced on her, she thought bitterly, this agony of sharing horrible circumstances with someone who couldn't cope: always having to supply the comfort and confidence she did not feel herself.

By and by, Verity's crying subsided. Anna wrapped a blanket round her. She brought the water over and laid the packet of fish and chips beside her. This time she was careful not to encourage her to eat. She was worried about the water. Roll had forgotten to fill the bucket or throw out the slops so there were only a couple of pints left.

When Verity's attention was focused on the food, Anna tore a square of toilet-paper off the roll and looked around for the piece of glass Lester had thrown. She found it near the reeking slop bowl, and carefully she picked it up, wrapped it, and stowed it in the pocket of her jeans.

CHAPTER 19

Bernie walked up the stairs to the office. It was six-thirty, cold and wet. No one could tell if he was tired or not as he ended even the most strenuous days at the same easy pace he began them. He released his energy in a steady stream like a Channel swimmer. Even his best friends could not pretend he was a sprinter.

At the top, he greeted Beryl who was showing signs of wear. Her tightly permed indigo hair looked lanker than usual and she had not repaired the make-up round her nose, which was thinned to a pink glaze by hay fever.

'Back from St John's Wood?' she said, brightly enough. Beryl could always state the obvious brightly. 'Mr Crocker's waiting in the rec-room and the Commander wants to see you both toot sweet.'

'In a minute,' Bernie said. 'First, I need an outside line and a cup of tea. Only then will I be ready for Mr Brierly.'

'You and your cups of tea,' Beryl said, smiling. She collected other people's foibles like snapshots. It was what she recognized them by. 'But don't be long. There've been Developments.'

In the rec-room, Bernie found Johnny in a mood of deep depression over the racing results in the evening paper. For once a hot tip had come good and he had failed to put money on it. There was tea in the pot though, and Bernie poured himself a mugful and stirred in two heaped teaspoons of sugar. He took a sip and sighed with pleasure.

Johnny said, 'Got the little bugger clapped in irons, eh?'

'A lot of good that does,' Bernie said, sitting down and dragging the phone towards him. 'I never knew anyone with so little to say and so many words to say it in. Got us nowhere, he has.'

'At least it's got the police running round the same track as us.'

'That's true,' Bernie said. 'Now I've got to phone the wife. We went and left poor old Phil out in the cold and I expect he'll've got in touch with her if there's anything doing.'

He dialled the number. Sylvia said, 'Hello, dear. Will you be in for supper?'

'Not till late,' Bernie said.

'Well, I'll keep you something warm. It's a nasty old evening.' Having completed what to her mind was essential, she went on, 'Phil Maitland phoned, dear, and said to tell you he'd been to those addresses you gave him. He said he'd had no luck. I'm sorry, dear.'

'That's all right,' Bernie said, rubbing the back of his neck. 'I didn't expect anything much. We had to try though.'

'He says he's back home now, and will you ring him there? He met a couple of men who want to talk to you.'

'Fine,' Bernie said, 'I'll do that. Thank you, Syl.' They chatted for a couple of minutes and then Bernie hung up.

'Sylvia sends her love,' he said, finishing his tea, and getting up to pour some more.

'What a woman,' Johnny said automatically, with his usual mixture of contempt and envy.

Bernie dialled again. 'Apparently Phil met someone,' he said as he waited for Phil to answer.

'Who?' Johnny asked.

'Don't know yet.' Bernie took another gulp from his mug. 'Phil? Yes, Bernie. What's the shout?'

'Well, squire,' Phil said, sounding as if Bernie had caught him in the middle of a mouthful of something tasty, 'I don't know what to make of it. I stumbled over these two bleeders who came across like the Trade Union Congress. A *Mister* Bates and a *Mister* Dunwoody.'

'That's right,' Bernie said. 'Willy's hoppos. I told you we might pass them in the night.'

'Well, in passing, they suggested you might like to participate in a full, frank exchange of views.'

'What?' Bernie asked.

'I told you,' Phil said, 'they was like a pair of shop stewards. Get around a table, all that malarky.'

'Oh, right,' Bernie said. 'When and where?'

'The Laundry,' Phil told him. 'Anytime till oh four hundred.'

'OK,' Bernie said.

'I'll come along, if you want a minder,' Phil offered.

'No need,' Bernie said. 'Thanks, but it isn't hairy.'

'They aren't a couple of pooftas,' Phil warned.

'No, but it isn't the occasion for funny stuff either,' Bernie said. 'Any other news?'

'I saw Pete's mother and she hasn't seen the little twit for three weeks. And I saw his stepmother and she hasn't seen him either. If you ask me, he's one of the least popular boys in town. It's funny, though, isn't it, them just going to ground like that. I mean, no one seems to've seen hide or hair.'

Bernie agreed and rang off. Then he and Johnny went down the corridor to Brierly's office. Beryl was already there, perched efficiently on a hard chair, notebook at half-mast, and one of her lethal yellow pencils aimed aggressively.

'Gentlemen,' Mr Brierly said, balancing his steel ruler on one thumb. 'A fine piece of work. I congratulate you.'

Bernie and Johnny exchanged a hurried glance and sat down. Bernie said, 'Not as productive as we'd hoped.'

'Nevertheless, a hunch that proved correct,' Mr Brierly said complacently. 'The police now have everything in hand, with a little help from us. And we can relax. As I say, a fine piece of work. It hasn't done us any harm with the authorities, none at all.'

'Quid pro quo?' Bernie asked mildly.

'Ah yes,' Mr Brierly said, laying the ruler on the desk in front of him. 'A tape-recording. I listened to it over the phone. A message from the girl to her father and a demand for ten thousand pounds plus an assurance that Mr Hewit will not give evidence against William Dutch. It's as we expected. Miss Doyle will give you a transcript.'

Beryl handed them a crisp sheet of paper. ' "We're being treated well",' Bernie read aloud. 'We. That's a relief. But ten thousand pounds?'

'Ridiculous, isn't it?' Mr Brierly said. 'Complete amateurs, as we suspected. It should be plain sailing from now on.'

'There isn't much time,' Bernie pointed out. 'Wednesday, they say. And there isn't much of Monday left now. What are the Hewits going to do?'

'I believe they are trying to raise the money now,' Brierly said vaguely, 'but I doubt if it'll come to that. Although, of course, the police want to be ready for any eventuality.'

'How was the tape delivered?' Johnny asked.

'Plain brown envelope through the letter-box at about five-thirty this afternoon. Mr Hewit informed the authorities immediately, sensible chap.'

'Wasn't the Hewit house being watched?' Bernie asked incredulously.

'Ah yes, but you know, rush hour,' Mr Brierly said distractedly. 'They admit to having slipped up there.'

'And the tape?'

'Somewhat amusing. The message was recorded over music by a pop group called the Pink, er Pink . . .'

'Floyd,' Beryl said flatly.

'Quite so. Anyway, an old cassette, sold in its thousands. There were no fingerprints, of course. These people can get something right, it seems.'

There was a moment's silence while Bernie and Johnny studied the transcript. Johnny said, ' "Instructions will come by phone." '

'All in hand. Listeners have been installed. So there you are, gentlemen, all we have to do now is wait. We will be informed of every new development as it happens. I am in close touch.'

'It's lovely to get back to normal,' Beryl said.

'Not quite normal,' Bernie reminded.

'Yes, well, I've no doubt Miss Lee will be back with us shortly,' Mr Brierly said. 'And that reminds me. I received an extraordinary phone-call from someone who claims to be a friend of hers. He says he's from the American Embassy and threatens an international incident unless we get a move-on. Mr Schiller?'

'Yes,' Bernie said resignedly, 'Gene Kovacs. I'll talk to him.'

'And that Chinaman,' Beryl added.

'Mr Minh isn't Chinese.' Bernie sighed. 'I'll get on to him too.'

'Well, I think that's all,' Mr Brierly said, getting to his feet and ushering Bernie and Johnny to the door. 'I am really most satisfied, most satisfied.'

They found themselves out on the High Street, hands in pockets, collars turned up. Johnny hunched his shoulders and said, 'Well, well. That seems to be that, doesn't it? You didn't leave anything up your sleeve, did you?'

'No,' Bernie said. 'Did you?' Johnny shook his head. 'All the same,' Bernie went on, 'I think I'll take another crack at Yvonne Wilson. She should be back from Brighton now.'

'Better leave it to the First Team,' Johnny said.

'They probably won't get round to it till the morning,' Bernie said, 'and I'd like to keep the momentum going.'

'Want a Man Friday?' Johnny asked.

'I don't think so. You get off home now, why not? One of us has to be fit for Beryl in the morning.'

They swapped goodnights and Bernie walked away through the rain to find his car.

When Verity had fallen into hunched exhausted sleep, Anna took the mutilated spring from its hiding place under the mattress and crept to the door. The grey

afternoon drizzle had given way to chilly evening. But
there was just enough light to see by. She knelt on the cold
floor and started to work on the lock.

Within an hour, she had unlocked and locked it three
times. After two hours, she could do it in two minutes
with her eyes closed. It was not much of an achievement
to unlock a firmly bolted door. But it was the only thing
she had accomplished in three days, so she had to be
satisfied.

Verity moaned, and even in her sleep her teeth
chattered. Anna went back to bed.

CHAPTER 20

Nothing had changed since the morning; or at least what
Bernie could see of it hadn't changed. Most of the light-
bulbs were broken and he climbed the stairs in twenty-
five-watt semi-blindness, pausing on each landing for a
breather. At the fifth, a lonely surviving lamp illuminated
a message that read 'Remember Brixton, Look Out
Kilburn' which looked as if it had been written in
manure. The eye-watering smell of urine hung in the
corners.

Yvonne Wilson's door was half open. Bernie stopped
and looked round. The corridor was empty. The flat was
dark and silent. He went in slowly and started turning on
lights. In the sitting-room a chair was overturned, and a
cup and saucer lay broken on the lino, the contents
soaking into the rug that lay skewed and rucked nearby.
That was the only sign of disturbance. There was not
much there to break anyway, just two more chairs and a
television set.

The bathroom was tiny and had the black mould of
condensation on the walls. The bath, basin, and lavatory

were dirty, and there was no one in there.

There was no one in the kitchen either. Bernie didn't spend long in it. It was in such confusion that the table lying on its side and the fallen sugar and sauce bottles on the floor hardly looked out of place.

He opened the bedroom door. Behind the wrecked bed, two stockinged feet poked out, splayed at ten to two. He had to step on tangled blankets to get to her. She lay on her back, large belly pointing at the ceiling, skirt screwed around her legs. Her face was covered in blood.

Bernie sat on the bed and picked up one of the limp hands. The fingers tightened on his and the bloody face gave a loud sniff.

'Yvonne?' Bernie said. His voice sounded loud and hoarse.

'I've got an awful nose-bleed,' she said thickly. 'Who the hell are you?'

'Wait a minute,' Bernie said, getting stiffly to his feet. He went to the bathroom and soaked a grimy striped towel in cold water, wrung it out and brought it back to the bedroom.

Even when he had cleaned the blood off her face, Yvonne still looked awful. Her nose was puffy and crusted round the nostrils, and both her eyes were nearly closed by purple swellings. Bernie looked around for something clean, and in the absence gave her his own handkerchief to hold to her nose, while he pressed the wet towel on the back of her neck. The bleeding slowed to a weary drip.

'Feeling better?' he said after a while.

'Yeah, ta,' she said from behind the handkerchief. 'I could do with a drink of water though. I've swallowed that much blood and it doesn't half taste rotten.'

He rinsed a sticky glass in the kitchen and brought it back to her. She got up off the floor and sat beside him on the bed. She said, 'What you doing here anyway?'

'I was looking for your brother, Pete, or Gary Natt.'

'What, you an' all?' she said, looking closely at him for the first time, out of one eye that looked like a slit in a squash ball. 'You a copper? You look like a copper.'

'Not anymore.'

'Well, you look like one,' she said again.

'Who else was here?'

'Mr Bates was here when I come home,' she said, sniffing loudly. 'Mr Bates. Master Bates, I call him. Get it?' She nudged Bernie and he smiled obligingly. 'Him and that other one. They go about together. I told them I didn't know nothing. I just got home, see?'

'Didn't they believe you?' Bernie asked sympathetically. 'Is that why they knocked you about?'

' 'Course not,' she said, surprised. 'They never laid a finger on me.'

'Who, then?'

'Bleeding Gary,' she said, as if it was obvious. 'He's a swine sometimes. Can you pass me hairbrush? I feel ever so clatty.' She brushed her lank brown hair, but it was so badly cut that it didn't look much better when she had finished. 'Having a baby makes your hair go funny, dunnit?'

'It looks all right,' Bernie said gallantly. 'Why did Gary hit you?'

'Oh, he's got an awful temper sometimes. He just don't like me talking to Mr Bates and that other one.'

'How well do you know Mr Bates?' Bernie asked.

'I just met him a couple of times when I was going with Gary,' she said. 'He's got a club in Battersea. Posh. I thought him and Gary was mates. Here, you got a fag or something?'

Bernie lit her a cigarette. He said, 'You shouldn't be smoking, you know. You ought to look after yourself more. You could lose the baby with all this going on.'

'What, this?' She patted her stomach with one hand while picking crusty blood out of her nose with the other.

'Fat chance. Don't think I didn't try. But I twigged too late, see, and the doctors wouldn't help.'

Bernie tried again. 'What exactly did you say to Gary that got him so angry?'

'You don't have to say much, do you?' She considered the question. It took her several minutes. Eventually she said, 'Here, he's in bother again, isn't he? What's he done this time?'

'Kidnapped two girls,' Bernie said shortly, 'him and your brother, and Jack Hardaker and Eric Tozer.'

'Pete?' she said, amazed. 'He couldn't kidnap pudding. He's a bit slow, see.'

'And the others?'

'Oh, Jack's all right. When he isn't stoned. I don't know any Erics.'

Bernie tried again. 'What did you tell Gary, about Mr Bates, I mean?'

'I can't remember exactly.' She thought for a while. 'Just that he was here, looking for him. And I said he might be at his mum's in Camberwell.'

'And then he hit you?'

'No, that wasn't it really,' she said. 'He did get a bit upset, mind you. No, what it was, was me asking for money. I'm broke, see, and me Giro don't come till Thursday.'

Bernie gave up. He said, 'Look, have you got a friend I can phone to help you get straightened out?'

'What for?' she said, gazing uncomprehendingly around at the mess. 'I don't have no phone.'

Bernie sighed and got up. He helped her make the bed and then went around picking up tables and chairs and broken crockery. He even made a cup of tea with a teabag and powdered milk while she got undressed. 'Look here, Yvonne,' he said, when he took it in to her, 'just stay put, will you. Don't open your door to anyone else tonight, all right?'

'OK,' she said cheerfully. She was sitting up in bed, her ruined face clashing horribly with a yellow nylon nightdress. 'You don't have a couple of quid spare, do you? I'm skint. I'll pay you back when the Giro comes.'

Bernie gave her some money, and she stuffed it under her pillow. 'That's nice of you,' she said. 'You may look like a copper, but you don't act like one.' She giggled as he prepared to leave. As he opened the front door, he heard her say, 'He don't act like one,' and another giggle. He took a few deep breaths and walked away. There was just one more errand before he could go home to Sylvia and 'something warm'.

Anna was asleep. She dreamed she owned a shop that sold second-hand doors. They stood in racks of ten, like paintings: doors of all sizes, shapes, and thickness: glass doors, wooden doors, steel doors, patio doors, fire doors, doors for ovens and refrigerators. At the counter was a fine display of hinges, keys, and bolts. Prominent among the keys was a huge gothic one, the sort that would open Castle Dracula. She did not want to sell this key. She knew it would come in handy soon. The shop was called The Slammer. Anna smiled in her sleep and turned over.

CHAPTER 21

Although known to the informed on both sides of the law as 'The Laundry', Willy Dutch's night-club was actually called The Flying Dutchman. It had a gaming licence, the club having been set up long before Willy acquired the property and took over the club, licence and all. But that was Willy's way. His eye would fasten on a concern that was wilting and then, like a pin-striped cuckoo, he would lay his egg of much-needed cash, accepting only a lot of gratitude and a few controlling shares in return. Then he would wait. And lo and behold, from his modest contribution, a full-fledged cuckoo would emerge and, after a while, Willy would find himself in sole occupancy of the nest. It made no difference to him if the nest were a garage, a pawnbroker's, or a firm that put up scaffolding: property was property and he had a use for everything.

The Flying Dutchman represented Willy's first foray into legitimate business. It was his lucky piece, and over the years little had changed, so that by now it had passed unchecked from gaudy to faded to shabby. But it still kept its place in his affections, and was the headquarters of his Old Guard. Bernie could remember when the crimson flocked wallpaper had been bright and proud. Now it was almost bald and the carpets had been worn into threadbare paths between the tables. A lonely man in a shiny dinner jacket was doing something atonal to 'Red Sails in the Sunset' on a baby grand, largely unnoticed by the few tired punters.

Bernie followed a redhead in green satin to the office behind the stage. The redhead had brown eyebrows and the green satin number was a size 16. It was a low-flying Dutchman these days, Bernie reflected, as he walked in to find the management ignoring their own facilities and engaged in a game of poker. No coloured plastic chips for them, just hard cash out on the table where everyone could see it.

'Hullo, Mr Schiller,' Dunwoody said, getting up. 'Nice to see you. Anno domini been treating you well, then?' Bates rose too, and said, 'Come into the inner sanctum and take the weight off.'

Bernie nodded affably to the two remaining poker-players and went through to the office. This was dominated by a modern Swedish bar and a leather-topped Victorian desk. A massive television set competed for attention with half a dozen Stubbs reproductions, but the rose-coloured armchairs were inviting, and Bernie sat down in one with a sigh of relief.

'Scotch, Mr Schiller?' Bates asked, holding a cut glass decanter in one hand and a plastic tumbler in the other.

'Well, Curly.' Bernie accepted his drink. 'It's been a long time. I hear you've had a spot of bother.'

'Straight to the point as usual, Mr Schiller,' Bates said, filling glasses for himself and Dunwoody. 'And we're anxious to avoid any more.'

'Which is why we invited you along, Mr Schiller,' Dunwoody added.

'We've been overlapping all day,' Bernie began.

'What you could call an interface situation,' Dunwoody agreed. 'But we did hear you got ahead of us this afternoon and picked up a young man not unconnected with our mutual interest.'

'You do hear well.'

'We still have our connections,' Bates said. 'But we'd be interested to hear from you if there've been any developments arising.'

'I'm wondering,' Bernie said slowly, 'why you should be so anxious. Surely, now that Gary Natt is firmly in the frame, you are firmly out of it.'

'That rather depends on what the little bastard says when you nail him,' Bates said with unusual directness.

'If there's any pinning done,' Dunwoody put in, 'we'd appreciate it if it wasn't on us.'

'That's hardly likely,' Bernie said. 'Gary Natt is not associated with you. That's well known.'

'It could be arranged though,' Dunwoody said.

'I don't think so,' Bernie said firmly. Bates and Dunwoody exchanged a swift glance. Then Bates said delicately, 'Not by you, believe me, I didn't mean that. But as you might've heard, there's been some friction.'

'A family dispute, so to speak,' Dunwoody added, turning away to top up his glass.

'And while the head of the family is elsewhere,' Bates continued, 'a certain person might use the opportunities to make sure the throne remains permanently his own.'

'I take it you're talking about young Carl,' Bernie said.

'We are referring to him, yes,' Bates said, embarrassed.

'There is,' Dunwoody said, 'a sort of generation gap situation.'

'Let me get this clear,' Bernie said thoughtfully. 'You are afraid that Carl might manipulate the circumstances to make you look bad.'

'We are anxious not to be implicated, yes,' said Bates.

'It is not insignificant that while the heat's been on us, the click around Carl has been more or less unharassed,' said Dunwoody.

'You've heard, of course, that a tape was delivered to Roly Hewit, threatening that if he testifies against Willy, his daughter will come to harm.'

'We have heard that, yes,' Dunwoody admitted.

'Well, isn't that what you want?'

'I think you've misunderstood, Mr Schiller,' Dunwoody said. 'All the tape does is dig a deeper hole for Willy. It's counter-productive.'

'The police already have Roly's evidence,' Bates said. 'So the tactics are clumsy and the timing couldn't be worse. Willy is most upset about it, and so's his brief.'

'I'd like to kick that little bastard's balls right up his backbone,' Dunwoody said, with sudden malevolence. 'He's tipped us right in it this time.'

Bernie said quickly, 'All I'm interested in is getting the hostages back unharmed and as quickly as possible.'

'We understand that,' Bates said, putting a restraining hand on Dunwoody's arm, 'and that is the conclusion we've been working to effect.'

'I'd like to be able to rely on that,' Bernie said. 'We've only got a day and a half.'

'You can, Mr Schiller,' Bates said, 'and in return, we'd

like you to bear in mind our position in all this.'

'We would not be ungrateful,' Dunwoody said, having recovered his poise.

'We understand each other then?' Bernie asked.

'I hope so, Mr Schiller,' said Bates.

'All the same,' Bernie mused, 'it's funny how Gary Natt has dropped so completely out of sight. It's almost as if he's had some help in all this. He doesn't have the reputation for being so clever.'

'He's a moron,' Bates said soothingly. 'If any of us could think like a moron, we'd've found him yesterday.'

'Nevertheless, there's four of them to hide,' Bernie said. 'Four of them needing food, drink and a bed for the night. Plus accommodation for two girls. Someone's subsidizing them.'

'Not necessarily,' Bates said.

Just then the redhead poked her head in and said she wanted to close the bar. It was very late. Bernie said goodnight and went out into the deserted dawn to drive home.

Anna woke with a start. The cats were fighting again, their snarls and screams disrupting the glum dawn. It was cold. She could just see her own breath wisping away into the half-light. What was even worse, she thought she could smell it too. Counting back, she realized with disgust that she hadn't cleaned her teeth since Saturday morning.

She got up quietly and squatted over the slop bowl. That steamed and smelled too. It was interesting, she thought, how in the end the unpleasant minor details had come to outweigh the major problems. There were times when it seemed more important to pee in privacy and keep your underwear clean than it was to escape, or work on schemes to keep yourself safe. It was humiliating and depressing.

She went back to bed, moving softly so as not to disturb Verity. She was glad that however upset Verity might get during the day, she always slept soundly at night. In fact, Verity's misery seemed to have a more lasting effect on Anna than it did on Verity herself. She came out of it purged and tired, while Anna was left feeling guilty and responsible.

After all, was it so important to stand up and talk back? Anna felt the danger of acquiescing very keenly indeed, but wasn't upsetting Verity even worse? Or was upsetting Verity only a small price to pay for her self-respect? And if Anna didn't stand up to them, what further liberties would their captors take?

She curled up behind Verity and tried to get back to sleep. She didn't know how long she could keep fighting on two fronts, or even whether it was worth it, but certainly she didn't want to face the morning on only a couple of hours' disturbed sleep.

CHAPTER 22

'There's a great furry spider patrolling the bottom of my bath,' Selwyn growled indignantly from the bathroom door.

'Wash it down the plughole, silly,' Bea mumbled, her head still under the duvet.

'Have you no respect for arachnids?' Selwyn asked. 'Anyway it's too big and it's got eyes like a blood-crazed leopard.'

'What's the time?' Bea said, peering cautiously at the alarm clock. 'Oh, Selwyn! It's only seven o'clock. You know I don't wake up till eight.' She pulled the duvet back over her head.

'I couldn't sleep,' Selwyn said crossly. 'And then I

wanted a bath. And now I can't.'

'Get Anna,' Bea murmured sleepily, 'she's good with spiders.' There was a short silence. Then Bea turned over and sat up. 'Oh dear,' she said. 'I forgot.'

'It's bloody insensitive you are,' Selwyn said. 'Why do you think I've become a raving insomniac? And what about my bath?'

'Pick the bloody spider up and put it out the window,' Bea said. 'That's what Anna does.'

'Well, I'm not Anna,' Selwyn said, shuddering. 'I'm a delicate chap with a vivid imagination, not a great white hunter. You do it.'

'Selwyn!' Bea sighed. 'It's only a spider.'

'That's right,' Selwyn said encouragingly. 'So you put it out the window. I'll make you a cup of coffee.'

'Bribery won't work either,' Bea yawned.

'You're scared,' Selwyn crowed.

'You're right.'

'If you don't do something, we'll never be able to use that bath again,' he pointed out. 'The spider'll move all its family in. And its furniture. That bath will become its permanent address, and all because you're too much of a coward to evict it.'

'What do you mean, I'm a coward?' Bea cried. 'What about you? You're the man of the house, and you're supposed to be brave and do all the things that need nerve. Has it occurred to you how much you rely on Anna to do all the things any self-respecting man'd do without turning a hair? Mum was right. I should've married Andy Davies.'

'That tedious little shop-keeper!' Selwyn said furiously. 'You'd've been bored out of your skull after a month.'

'You're right,' Bea sighed again and swung her legs off the bed. 'Try and remember how Anna got rid of that wasp you wouldn't let me kill.'

'She put a glass over it and slid a piece of paper under

it,' Selwyn said. 'That's a good idea. I'll get you a glass.'

Before he opened his eyes, Bernie knew there were kippers for breakfast. He lingered in bed for a few minutes to sharpen his appetite. Sylvia's kippers were a great delicacy for Bernie, a delicacy that was largely unappreciated by the younger members of the Schiller household. Sheer prejudice, Bernie thought, what could beat a good kipper on a dull rainy morning? Then he looked at the clock and found it was half-past nine. He washed and shaved hurriedly and went down to the kitchen knotting his tie.

'I've already phoned the office,' Sylvia said without turning away from her fragrant frying-pan, 'so they aren't expecting you till ten-thirty. You came in so late last night, you needed the lie-in.'

'Any news?' Bernie asked, sitting down. 'That smells wonderful.'

'I thought it'd wake you up.' Sylvia smiled at him fondly.

'Better than the alarm clock,' Bernie said. 'What's the news?'

'None, I'm afraid,' Sylvia said, sliding the kippers on to a hot plate with crisp triangles of buttered toast. She put them in front of him like a consolation prize. 'Don't let it spoil your food.'

Bernie didn't. If he knew about anything, it was how to take events one at a time and not let his worries interfere with his digestion. People with ulcers didn't last long in his business.

When he had finished he went into the hall and made three phone calls. The first was to Mr Minh. He told him that Anna was away and would call him as soon as she got back. Mr Minh sounded relieved. The second was to an old CID friend, and the third was to Gene Kovacs.

'What the hell is going on?' Gene said. 'I keep calling

your office and all I get is some receptionist who won't tell me squat, even when I said I was from the Embassy.'

'That wouldn't impress Beryl,' Bernie told him, 'even if it was true.'

'Well, I had to say something to get her off her butt,' Gene said impatiently. 'Look, we haven't met, but Anna's told me a lot about you. So how about some straight answers?'

'I'll try,' Bernie said, amused. Women like Beryl simply did not possess butts. 'But there really isn't any news yet. The police know who they're looking for now, and it's a question of routine work, door to door with photographs.'

'How do they know where to look?' Gene asked. 'These guys might be in the middle of Romney Marsh for all we know.'

'One of them surfaced yesterday. Went to see his girl-friend, which leads everyone to suppose they're some-where in South London. Lambeth, most like. The police are keeping an eye on all the families and friends in case one of them pops up again.'

'That's all very fine,' Gene exclaimed, 'but suppose none of them does "pop up", how long've we got? There's always a deadline.'

'Wednesday afternoon,' Bernie said calmly.

'That's tomorrow!' Gene said loudly. 'Shit, what's everyone messing around for?'

'From a kidnapper's point of view, that's the most difficult time. It's when things are most likely to go wrong and they're most likely to be caught.'

'And when the victims are most likely to get fried if anyone screws up,' Gene said aggressively.

'I've just been talking to someone in CID,' Bernie said mildly, 'and all sorts of arrangements have been made. I can't tell you what, at present, but there are procedures, Mr Kovacs, that have proved successful in the past.'

'Procedures!' Bernie held the phone away from his ear

to protect his eardrums. Even Sylvia, who had come to the kitchen door to listen, looked startled.

'Listen,' Bernie said when he had the chance. 'I know you're worried, but I'm just trying to tell you that everything's being done that can be done, and you won't help anyone by getting frantic.'

'And you won't help anyone by quoting police procedure like Grandpa Moses,' Gene said.

'He sounds homesick,' Bernie said as he rang off hurriedly. 'I was just trying to reassure him but I don't think I succeeded.'

'Never mind,' Sylvia said, going back to the stove. 'Americans are very excitable people.'

'All the same,' Bernie said slowly, 'waiting isn't easy. I know how he feels. Just when it's getting a bit urgent, there's nothing left for me to do either.'

Sylvia looked at him thoughtfully. 'If I were you,' she said eventually, 'I'd go back and talk to that boy Henry, if you haven't heard anything by lunch-time. Maybe there's somewhere they used to go when they were children and wanted to hide. People don't break old habits in a crisis. In fact that's when they rely on them most.'

'He'll've been pumped dry by now,' Bernie said. 'Still, there's no harm trying.'

'It'll ease your mind,' Sylvia said, putting the breakfast dishes in a plastic bowl.

'It might,' Bernie said. 'Another thing I'd like to do is get hold of Carl Dutch. There's something there I can't put my finger on.'

So Bernie made his fourth phone call of the morning to find out where he might find Carl Dutch. It was only a remote possibility that Carl had anything at all to do with Verity Hewit's disappearance. Unless he was very stupid he must know that, far from helping his father, such a crude attempt at pressuring Roly Hewit would actively harm him. And although Carl might benefit from his father's absence, Bernie could not believe that he would try to make matters worse. On the other hand, Carl was indeed making hay and Willy Dutch's corporation was split down the middle. Those who were loyal to Willy were doing their best to prevent themselves from being implicated, while Carl seemed curiously unaffected.

Another thing that puzzled Bernie was how passive Willy himself was. As Bernie remembered him, Willy had been a man of vast energy who kept an army of briefs to deal with any trouble, and who could call on a similar number of foot-soldiers to do his dirty work, or provide him with alibis if he ever needed to do it himself. He was the ideal scout who was always prepared, always had a safety net. Of course, he had been nicked before. He had even done time long ago. But Bernie could not remember an occasion when he had been caught with his guard down, as he had when Reub Irving died.

According to Bernie's friend, who knew the case well, Willy had simply denied being out that afternoon. And according to the same source, there had been no one apart from his wife to back him up. 'It's two deaths really, mate,' Bernie's friend said. 'Reub Irving's murder and Willy's suicide.' Bernie's friend was one of Willy's oldest adversaries, but even he sounded almost regretful. 'It's not like him,' he went on, 'not at all. If you ask me he must've had an eppi-fit. Normally he prepares his defence *before* he does a naughty. This time he's in arrears.'

'He used to be very close to Reub,' Bernie reminded him. 'Perhaps it was Reub betraying him . . .'

'Bit of a crime of passion? I thought that myself,' his friend agreed. 'I knew we'd clobber him proper one day, but it's sad him going down without a fight. He's a broken man, Bernie, old son. Not like when you and me played Cowboys and Indians with him. Says he was watching the racing on telly when Reub got hit. Can you credit it?'

Bernie couldn't. And he didn't give it much thought

for the rest of the morning either. He spent that running down a luckless mechanic who had given up his digs in order to avoid the finance company which wanted its caravan back. He hadn't gone far, and his wife's mother told Bernie where to find him with uncharitable speed. Instead of reporting back to Beryl with the good news, Bernie pointed his car towards the Elephant and Castle.

'You were dreaming,' Verity said. 'You twitch like a cat when you're dreaming.'

'Was I?' Anna said, sitting up and rubbing her eyes. 'I didn't mean to go to sleep at all. I hate sleeping in the middle of the day.'

'What were you dreaming about?' Verity asked, sitting on the end of the bed.

'I was looking for someone,' Anna said vaguely. Actually, the dream depressed her so badly that she didn't want to talk about it. She had been at home when the BBC gave out an announcement. In matter of fact tones, the news reader said that there was about to be a nuclear explosion. Death would be inevitable, but horrible and lingering unless every member of the public could find a partner to die with. Two people, holding each other tightly, would concentrate the rays in such a way that death would be quick and painless. 'Good luck and God bless,' said the announcer before he went off the air to the strains of the National Anthem. Anna rushed downstairs to find Selwyn, but Bea was home from work and they were already locked in their final embrace. In a panic she ran out into the street looking for someone to die with. She saw Gene, but as she hurried towards him a blonde woman opened a taxi door and drew him in with her. They drove away together. Everywhere couples stood or lay hugging each other. Anna kept running, looking around desperately for a partner. She went to Holland Park, and there, at the far end of an avenue of lime trees, she saw Verity walking by herself, unaware of the danger. 'Over here!' Anna shrieked, but there was a loud rumbling like thunder in the sky and Verity did not hear. Anna raced towards her, calling frantically. When only a few yards separated them, the explosion came. There was a flash of white light and the tree tops burst into flame. Anna knew she was too late.

'Who were you looking for?' Verity asked.

'I think it was you,' Anna said.

'Where were you looking?' Verity asked, interested.

'In Holland Park.'

'Did you find me?'

'Yes,' said Anna, pulling herself together.

'Does that mean, deep down inside, you're worried about me?'

'I expect so,' Anna said uncertainly. She did not like to interpret dreams, because she felt, rather, that dreams interpreted her.

'Well, I've never been to Holland Park,' Verity said, looking pleased. 'When do you think they'll bring our lunch? I'm starving.'

CHAPTER 23

The Paragon Club was in a big building overlooked by the London College of Printing. Bernie pushed through the glass doors and walked quickly past a counter, but not quickly enough to escape attention.

'Can I help you, sir?' A large man with brown ribbons of hair pasted over his scalp leaned across his desk.

'I'm looking for Carl Dutch,' Bernie said, reluctantly going back.

'Is he expecting you?' the man asked. 'I'm sorry, sir, but it's members only. Unless you're a guest.'

'He's expecting me,' Bernie said.

'Can I have your name, sir?'

'Schiller,' Bernie said, resignedly reaching for his wallet.

'I don't see it here, sir,' the man said, paying more attention to the cut of Bernie's suit than to the list in front of him. Bernie placed a tenner on the pages of the visitors' book.

'Do you see it now?' he asked.

'Upstairs. Door on your right,' said the man. The tenner disappeared. Bernie went up. He passed through another glass door into a large room with a low ceiling. In spite of the subdued spot-lighting, the place failed to be intimate. In fact it had all the cosiness of an airport lounge. A long bar ran along one wall and was serviced by three barmen in scarlet waistcoats. Above the bar was a large television showing a continuous CEEFAX display, so that members could entertain themselves with exchange rates and the hottest numbers on the stock market while waiting for their White Ladies and steak sandwiches. There was an air of well-tailored paranoia among the men, and the few women looked, too, as if their suits were from Savile Row and their anxieties from the City. Bernie felt like a lone pigeon in a flock of starlings.

He asked directions from a hostess and was answered with a shrug and a crimson smile. Yet another glass door divided the regulars from the snooker players. Bernie was stopped from entering by a club official. In a different suit and half a mile further south, he would have been a bouncer. Here, he was an assistant manager.

'Members only, sir,' he said, stepping smartly into Bernie's path. 'I'm sorry, sir, no guests, no dogs, and no women. There are only the two tables, you see.'

A woman sitting by herself at the end of the bar turned round and said, 'Give them an extra table, sweetheart. The dogs are breaking their hearts.'

'I'm looking for Mr Dutch,' Bernie said.

'He hasn't finished the frame,' said the assistant manager, glancing through the glass doors. 'If you'd like to give me your name, I'll tell him you're waiting.'

Bernie told the man his name and sat down on a stool next to the woman. Lined up in front of her in a tidy row were three glasses of a clear drink and three bottles of Britvic orange juice.

'They won't let the dogs play billiards and they won't let the dogs buy their own drinks,' she said, 'so don't tell me it's not a dog's life.' She pointed to the bottles and glasses and went on, 'This lot is an hour's worth. You can have one if you like. Carl takes time getting his pink into the top pocket.'

Bernie laughed. She had a face like an intelligent mouse with vast black eyes overshadowing a small pointed nose and an equally pointed chin. Her hair sprouted from her head like ruffled feathers. She looked as out of place as Bernie felt, and he told her so.

'Thank you,' she said seriously. 'Frankly, I prefer the unwashed to the undead, but the choice isn't mine. You see, I used to be a giraffes' brain surgeon, but I can't stand heights. Coming down in the world was a great relief. Also, giraffes have very small brains. Sometimes you climb all that way up and then you can't find the brain at all. And then, you know, my hands grew too big. Oh, it's tough at the top.'

'I like giraffes,' Bernie said softly. Her wayward conversation appealed to him today.

'Oh, so do I,' she said, 'and if they came a little shorter and bigger brained, I'd really love them.'

'Now, take the camel . . .' Bernie suggested.

'Ah, the camel.' She grinned from ear to ear. 'Now there's a job I'd like, chiropodist to a camel. Do you know, they have Dunlopillo in their feet and ankles? Just watch a string of camels cross the dunes at Margate.

You'd swear they were walking on a trampoline.'

They sat in silence for a few moments, contemplating the camel. Then Bernie turned sideways on his stool to look through the glass doors. 'Which one's Carl?' he asked. She turned too and pointed. 'The one with the Dracula wig,' she said, and Bernie picked out a slender man leaning on his cue. His dark hair was brushed straight back from a pronounced widow's peak, giving his face a shield shape. He looked up at that moment, saw her pointing and scowled.

'Oops,' she said, swinging back to the bar, 'another goof. Carl is so touchy. Never mind, if he thinks we're talking about him behind his back, he'll be out like a shot.'

'Pity. I was enjoying myself,' Bernie admitted truthfully.

'So was I. Although this is the last place on earth you'd think of to rediscover the Sierra Madre of conversation. Still, duty before pleasure.'

'What duty?' Bernie asked.

'I'm Carl's chauffeur. Or chauffeuse as Carl's mother so disgustingly puts it. Like masseuse. It makes me sound plural.'

'But what about all the booze?' Bernie said, surprised.

'Oh, that's just water,' she said airily. 'It's my keep-off-the-grass sign. Otherwise I get all the undead queueing up to buy me a proper drink, which is a pain in the aardvark. And since you didn't make any of the usual remarks about peaked caps and leather boots and suitable jobs for women, I'll tell you about it.'

'Don't risk your job,' Bernie said, suddenly feeling that he knew more about Carl's need for privacy than she did.

'What's to risk?' she asked. 'I like driving good cars, and Carl likes buying them. It's the basis of a perfect relationship.'

'All the same—' Bernie began.

'All the same, I do not like old men I have not invited coming into my club and questioning my employees.' Carl Dutch stood close behind them, polishing his cue with a soft leather cloth. His circumflex eyebrows gave him a look of disdainful surprise. Otherwise it was a closed and secretive face.

'He wasn't questioning me,' the woman said, puzzled.

'He wouldn't have to,' Carl said. 'Sometimes you run off at the mouth like a drain in a thunderstorm. Go and sit in the car.'

'She hasn't said anything,' Bernie said quickly.

'And she's not going to,' Carl said. 'Go and sit in the car.'

'Just a minute,' the woman said, standing up. 'You may pay my wages, but I can still talk to whoever I want to.'

'If you think that, my dear,' Carl said icily, 'perhaps I'd better stop paying your wages.'

'Perhaps you better had!' she said, her black eyes sparkling with anger. 'And don't call me "my dear". You're too young to be so patronizing.'

'Hold on,' Bernie said. 'This is plain foolish. I didn't ask her anything and she didn't volunteer anything either.'

'This is none of your business, old man,' Carl said. 'In fact, all my business is none of your business. Get it?' The assistant manager came over, attracted by the raised voices. 'Any trouble, Mr Dutch?' he asked eagerly.

'Who let this man in here? He is not my guest,' Carl said, turning on him.

'Must be some mistake,' the assistant manager said. 'I'm so sorry, sir.' He took hold of Bernie's sleeve. Bernie shook him off and stood up.

'Throw him out,' Carl said.

'Don't do that,' Bernie said mildly, shaking off the intrusive hand a second time, 'unless you're really addicted to hospital food.' He turned away and started for the door, the woman following.

'Not you,' Carl snapped, holding her back.

'Make up your mind,' she complained. 'I thought you wanted me to go.'

'Not with him,' Carl said.

'Then I'm not fired?' she asked sweetly.

'Of course not, my dear,' he said smoothly.

'Good. Then I resign. I told you not to call me "my dear".' With that, she hurried off after Bernie with Carl in hot pursuit. In the middle of the room she stopped and said in a piercing voice, 'Really, Mr Dutch. Touch me there again and I'll scream. It's a disgrace!' she informed the rest of the members who had turned to look, 'after what he did to my little sister. I'm surprised he has the nerve!'

Carl looked murderous and flushed to the roots of his hair. 'She's neurotic,' he said loudly.

'You see!' she cried happily. 'He's ruined my whole family.' She backed away. Carl looked as if he wanted to hit her, and Bernie took her arm and pulled her towards the door.

'You live dangerously,' he said, as they arrived breathless at the top of the stairs.

'Did you see that?' she cried as they started down. 'The great undead live! It's the scent of blood, you see. Makes the hair on the soles of their feet start curling. You'd better watch out, there's a full moon tonight.'

'So had you,' Bernie muttered as he led her across the lobby and out into the street.

'Christ,' she said, suddenly sobered by the fresh air, 'I'm unemployed. What am I going to do?'

'Where's Carl's car?' Bernie asked.

'In the underground car park,' she told him. 'Shall we go and rip it off? I've still got the keys. It's a Mercedes and worth a bomb.' She led the way down a ramp at the side of the building.

The car squatted like a steel toad, straddling two parking spaces. 'I never park straight,' she said proudly. 'It's a matter of exclusivity. I told Carl that. I said, "Anyone can have a chauffeur, but it takes a man of distinction to keep a bad one." '

Bernie took the keys and opened the doors. He searched the car quickly, but it was as clean and tidy as if it had never left the showroom, and he came up with nothing more telling than a pair of sunglasses. The woman watched him curiously.

'I know what,' she said when he had finished, 'let's lock the keys in the car. That'll bring him out in spots.'

'Let's not,' Bernie said firmly, and hid the keys neatly behind a rear wheel. 'Now, first things first: where do you live?'

'Oh dear,' she wailed, thoroughly crestfallen, 'I'm homeless too. I had the flat above the garage.'

'Well, you can't go back there,' Bernie said, starting to walk back to street level.

'Why not?' she asked running to catch up. 'He'll have to give me a week's notice at least.'

'You don't want to go back there,' Bernie repeated. 'You'd better come home with me. The boys are away for the summer so there's plenty of room.'

'Whoa!' she said. 'What's your game, mister?'

'White slaver,' Bernie replied, without turning around. 'Take it or leave it.'

'Why didn't you say so?' she said, relieved. 'I thought you were Salvation Army.'

Time shuffled by. An hour or so had passed since lunch, what there was of it. And something new had been added to Anna's anxiety. The lads were smug today: smug and alert. They must have delivered their message successfully, she thought. They seemed bloated with their success and hadn't even responded to her needling.

'There's negotiations,' Shake had said, full of self-importance. 'You'll see. You don't fuck with urban guerrillas.'

'No, you keep them in zoos where they belong,' Anna said, but that didn't puncture them at all.

Afterwards, she stripped the mattress off the bed and stood the bare frame under the window where she and Verity took it in turns shouting out to the unyielding wall beyond.

'It's a waste of time,' Verity complained hoarsely and Anna had to agree. They had shouted at various times every day without result. She examined the bedstead for the umpteenth time wondering how to turn it into a weapon. But without tools, the only removable bits were the springs. Doubled over, one of them might make a handy cosh, but it wouldn't be much use against four crash helmets. Anna removed one anyway.

'What's that for?' asked Verity, who had been mercifully uncurious about the other one that Anna had battered into a rudimentary key.

'Just in case,' Anna said vaguely. 'Let's play hopscotch.' She used the spring to scratch squares on the floor. Verity grumbled that she was too old for such childish games. But after some persuasion she joined in, and more time trudged by.

CHAPTER 24

'I like your husband,' Laura said to Sylvia while drinking tea, both hands around the cup in a way that reminded Bernie painfully of Anna. 'First, he gets me canned, then evicted, and now he's kidnapped me.'

'He's impulsive,' Sylvia said, glancing quickly at Bernie. 'Would you like some strudel with your tea?'

'Love some,' Laura said with enthusiasm. 'You know, it's funny, but before he ruined my life, I'd marked him out for a fisherman. I could just see him, up to his sartorius in burn water and wellies, stalking the elusive salmon.'

'Not bad,' Bernie said, rousing himself. 'Not bad at all.'

'Who'd've thought the patient angler could have provoked such poison in my ex-boss.' She rested her elbows on the butter-yellow tablecloth and regarded Bernie with admiration. 'Carl Dutch is usually as smooth as a silkworm. Do you know, he doesn't smoke, but he keeps a solid gold lighter in his pocket to impress the feather boa brigade. And cash! He has cash oozing from every pore. It made my eyes water. I used to have fantasies that he was a Tong paymaster or a Grandfather.'

'Godfather,' Bernie corrected her. 'And again, not bad. Did you ever meet his old man?'

'He's in Switzerland with a spot on his lung,' she said innocently. 'Now there's a paterfamilias, the sort that gave Oedipus his bad reputation. Carl grew to twice his normal size when old Mr D went away.'

'She's rather shrewd, isn't she?' Sylvia said to Bernie. 'She'd love you to think she was talking nothing but nonsense, but it doesn't quite work.'

'I'm up for adoption,' Laura said hopefully. 'My own mother doesn't understand me at all.'

'You surprise me,' Bernie said drily. 'Now, how would you like to sing for your supper?'

'I can give you Tosca, if supper's anywhere near as good as tea,' Laura answered promptly. 'Or my version of Moon River. It once brought all the crowned heads of Europe to their feet.'

'On their way to the exit, no doubt,' Bernie said. 'No, what I want to know is how you got your job with Carl, if you know anything about the accident which killed Reub Irving, and whether or not Carl has met or talked about some people called Gary Natt, Eric Tozer, Pete Wilson, and Jack Hardaker.'

'Why?' Laura asked baldly. 'No, don't tell me. You've got a kind face and I've decided to take you at face value.'

'Thank you,' said Sylvia quietly.

'So,' Laura went on, 'I can tell you without any fear of thirty pieces of silver that I have never heard any of the four names you mentioned nor have I seen them, unless unknowingly. Carl didn't usually introduce his friends to his driver. Also there was a glass panel in the car which he used to employ whenever my ears went pointy.

'As to the accident, well, that I believe was responsible for old Mr D's sojourn in "Switzerland". The man who was killed was Carl's Uncle Reuben. Carl's Dutch uncle I used to call him, because he had a very waggy finger. He was always saying, "Carl, you can't do that," or "Better ask your father" as if Carl were a small boy.

'The Mercedes really belongs to old Mr Dutch. It's the death car. But I didn't mind because the police had it hosed down thoroughly and it was a step up from the Audi Eighty.'

'Were you with Carl that day?' Bernie asked.

'No. Thursday was my day off. I got back to find pandas all over the lawn and old Mrs Dutch watering the begonias with her tears. Carl was spending the day with his girl-friend in Pinner and he didn't get home till later. It was all very dramatic. But I can't tell you much about it because I was given an unexpected Christmas bonus and sent packing to the flat chest of my family.

'When I came back, Carl was wearing a larger size in boots, and I was given the Merc to wheel his eminence around in. Old Mr Dutch had gone to take the waters in the Alps, I was told. A likely story, what with old Mrs D running off to Brixton every other day with a hamper, and all those lawyers coming round for tea and buns. I'm not as green as I'm cabbage-looking.'

Bernie and Sylvia looked at each other. There was a short silence while Laura munched a second piece of strudel. Then she said, 'The job was advertised in *The Times*, no less. I applied, largely because my father was on my back for being an overqualified layabout, and my mother kept dropping hints to the mathematician I was going out with at the time.' She paused while Sylvia refilled her cup. 'I've got an honours degree in History,' she explained, 'and I think it was that that clinched the job for me. I was puzzled at first, seeing that I've no experience as a chauffeur, but then I noticed the Dutch secret perversion.'

'What's that, dear?' Sylvia asked.

'They get a buzz out of employing lame Top People,' Laura said. 'Their au pair is an Austrian baroness. The cook used to be a pop star, before he had his nervous collapse, and the gardener is a bishop's younger son who took too much acid. Bizarre, don't you think?'

'Odd,' Bernie agreed. 'One more question. Has Carl talked about a kidnapping in the last few days?'

'No,' she said, 'although one of his cronies did. I was driving them to the golf-club on Sunday, and this friend of his said had he heard that Somebody Something's daughter had been hijacked.'

'What did Carl say?'

'Nothing. But he laughed like a kookaburra. He's got a funny sense of humour, I think.'

The phone rang, and Bernie went out to the hall to answer it. Johnny was phoning from the office. 'Phil and I are off home unless you've got any blacklegging for us.'

'No,' Bernie said reluctantly. 'It's gone cold on us. I thought I'd have another bash at H, but that's all. How's the Infantry getting on, by the way?'

'Last bulletin about an hour ago,' Johnny said. 'They're

out in force with photographs and descriptions, but the going's a bit soft.'

'Nothing, then?'

'They got all steamed up over a couple of sightings near Lambeth Palace, but it turned out the witnesses were unreliable. They identified the police surgeon as well.'

'Early days yet,' Bernie said. 'You and Phil might as well scarper. If I need troops, I'll call you at home. I'm off to see H now.'

'While you're at it, give the little pronk a sock in the eye from me,' Johnny said cheerfully and rang off.

Sylvia came out and joined Bernie in the hall. She picked up the clothes brush that hung on the coatrack and brushed the shoulders of his jacket. The gesture was very like a caress. After a while she said carefully, 'Carl Dutch is not the point. You're going off at a tangent. Leave it alone.'

Bernie smiled at her affectionately. 'I had an idea, but it was a bit farfetched, I admit.'

'I think it was half right and half wrong. But the right part won't find you Anna.'

'I agree,' he said thoughtfully. Sylvia relaxed. 'Good,' she said, giving his shoulders a final swipe with the brush. 'So, if Henry can't help, don't stop out till all hours and don't come home with any more orphaned chauffeurs. I can only cope with one at a time.'

The sun had come out now that it was too late to give anyone more than a little pleasure. Bernie fought the traffic to St John's Wood by way of a long detour to Victoria Street. Even so it saved time because his old friend at New Scotland Yard was able to pull the strings that opened Henry Ames's cell to him.

Henry was languishing, and it suited him. His long thin body drooped in disconsolation to the manner born. 'They can't keep me here,' he complained. 'I've told them everything I bleeding know.'

'Have you seen a solicitor?' Bernie asked.

'Lot of good that's done me. I'm still here, en' I? And who's going to break it to my Mum, eh? She'll be doing her nut.'

'I could drop in on her, if you want,' Bernie offered. He took a packet of Embassy out of his pocket and passed it to Henry.

'Tell her it weren't my fault,' Henry whined. 'After all, it was you got me in this bind.'

'It's the company you keep,' Bernie said. 'You ought to be a bit more clever about your friends.'

'You can say that again. It's them's done the job, but look who's in chokey. Typical.' His eyes glazed with tears of self-pity and Bernie got the distinct impression that he was enjoying himself.

'Where would they go, Henry?' he asked. 'Where's the bolthole?'

'Search me,' Henry said, lighting a cigarette and blowing a long stream of smoke at the ceiling.

'Only they've kept their heads down pretty successfully,' Bernie said. 'They must be cleverer than you thought.'

'Them! Clever!' Henry exclaimed, outraged.

'All the same,' Bernie insisted, 'they must be a bit canny to keep stum for so long.'

'I've got more brains in my sock than they've got put together,' Henry said angrily. 'They never got out of the D-stream at school. Me, I've got CSEs, I told you.'

'You did. But you're not at school now, and you don't need much of an education to be street-wise.'

'Scuffers! What do you know?' he said contemptuously. 'I could find them just like that!' He tried to snap his fingers, but his hands were sweating.

'I see,' Bernie said in polite disbelief. 'Very interesting. In that case, I wonder why you haven't tried to do a deal with the police. If Gary isn't found, you could end up with all his manure on your head.'

'A lot you know, then,' Henry said. 'I've got a good solicitor working on my case. And he says they can't prove a thing if I keep my mouth shut.'

'Oh well, if you really like police cells, there's not much I can do to help,' said Bernie, standing up. He picked up the packet of Embassy and put it back in his pocket. This seemed to disturb Henry.

'I told my solicitor everything,' he began uncertainly, 'and he said any deals to be done, he'd do it. It's safer that way. He knows his way around all right.'

'This solicitor,' Bernie said, making slowly for the door, 'are you sure he isn't working for Gary Natt?'

'What do you mean?' Henry said uncomfortably. Then he snorted and said, 'He wouldn't have Gary to clean his car for him. You can't put one over on me.'

'Silly of me,' Bernie said, knocking for the officer who was waiting outside. 'You're a smart lad, Henry.'

'You could leave the fags, though,' Henry said hopefully. 'No hard feelings? And you won't forget about my Mum?'

Outside in the corridor Bernie waited while the young constable locked the door. Then they walked together to the bottom of the stairs.

'Who's his brief?' Bernie asked before they parted.

'A Mr Box-Holtom,' the constable said, 'a real flower. He was here just before you. He wears high-heeled boots.'

'Legal Aid?' Bernie asked, starting up the stairs.

'Not on your life,' the young man said, 'but don't ask me who sent him.'

Bernie walked slowly up to the ground floor. The sergeant in charge of the desk let him look at the phone book for free, but he had to pay to use the phone. He looked at his watch while he waited for an answer. It was nearly seven-thirty.

'Box-Holtom-Associates-can-I-help-you,' said the

receptionist at the other end of the line. It was the voice of
a woman who is working late and wants everyone to know
what a sacrifice she's making.

'It's Clive Bates for Mr Box-Holtom,' Bernie said.

'Putting-you-through-Mr-Bates,' sang the receptionist.
After a few clicks and whirrs, an exquisite tenor voice
said, 'Mr Bates, how kind of you to call. I was just about
to get in touch with you.' Bernie hung up. He stared at
the desk sergeant who stared woodenly back. In the end
he said thoughtfully, 'I think someone ought to go and
talk to Henry Ames's solicitor. He's working for a man
who works for Willy Dutch. This man is also looking for
Gary Natt and his mates, and unless I'm very much
mistaken, Henry told him where to find them.'

The desk sergeant reached for the internal telephone
and spoke for a few minutes. Then he said, 'Why don't
you go and wait in the canteen, Mr Schiller. We may
need you in a little while.'

CHAPTER 25

Looking up at the darkening grey rectangle of the
window, Anna reckoned it was getting on for nine
o'clock. It was not cold that night, but Verity had
wrapped one of the paper-thin blankets round her and
was pacing up and down. There was only room for one of
them to pace comfortably at a time, so Anna sat crosslegged on the bed with her back against the wall. The
cellar room smelled, but at least the flies had gone home
to bed. Verity was hungry. She told Anna so at frequent
intervals. Anna's hunger was overwhelmed by her
increasing anxiety. The boys had not come, so there was
no food, hardly any fresh water, and the slop bucket,
unemptied, was spreading its sickening odour into the

four corners of the room.

Anna was convinced that something had gone wrong. The boys had set a pattern which was now broken. They had come twice a day so far: once at about midday, and again before dark. In such confined circumstances any break in routine seemed dramatic and ominous. What Anna feared most was that the boys had got into some trouble completely unconnected with her and Verity. She could imagine lads of that calibre being nicked for shoplifting, for instance, or crashing a stolen car. If that was the case, their connection with an obscure kidnapping might not be discovered for some time, and she and Verity would be left to rot. She had difficulty imagining a fate more unpleasant than starving slowly in a tiny stinking hole with a distraught teenage girl for company.

Anna's claustrophobia, well controlled until now, rose suddenly. Sweat broke out on her forehead, her lungs tightened and her hands shook with damp chill. She jumped off the bed and went to stand under the window to catch the cool down-draught.

Verity stopped her restless pacing and stood beside her. There were too many people in the cellar, Anna thought wildly, two too many. 'Let's move the bed under the window,' she said quickly, to prevent herself from climbing desperately on to Verity's shoulders to reach the broken window. 'It smells a bit better over here.'

'It'll be cold later on,' Verity said dubiously, 'and we'll have to move it back if it rains again.' But she heaved enthusiastically at the bed, glad to have something to do. 'When do you think they'll come?' she asked monotonously, panting from the exertion.

'I don't think they will now,' Anna replied levelly. 'We'll just have to wait till morning.'

'But suppose they don't come tomorrow either?'

How should I know? Anna wanted to scream. 'They'll

come, don't worry,' she said coolly. 'Do you know any memory games?'

'I went to the shop?' Verity suggested. Her face was now just a shadow in the gathering dark.

'Good idea,' Anna said encouragingly. 'You start.'

'I went to the shop and bought a tin of Heinz Baked Beans,' Verity began.

'I went to the shop and bought a tin of Heinz Baked Beans and a saddle for my fat donkey.'

Verity giggled. 'I went to the shop . . .' As the game progressed, they spread out the blankets and settled themselves comfortably under them. By and by, Verity grew sleepy and forgot the ball-peen hammer that Anna had inserted into the long catalogue of unlikely objects. 'You win,' she said yawning loudly. 'You've got an awfully good memory. I expect it's all that working in the library. I usually win this game at home.' She turned on her side and within a few minutes her breathing was deep and regular.

In the canteen Bernie snoozed peacefully. He sat in one easy chair with his feet up on another, a folded newspaper protecting his eyes from the glare of the strip lighting, completely undisturbed by the few officers who came and went for their late evening refreshments. Now and then a gentle snore escaped him and the young officers would look at each other and smile. He was the picture of relaxation, his hands loosely clasped across his paunch.

A young woman wearing a green velvet jacket and jeans came in. She started over towards Bernie, then changed her mind and went to the hot drinks machine instead, where she selected sweet milky coffee. She approached Bernie again and coughed politely. The paper slid from his face to his chest.

'DC Huxtable, sir,' the woman said. 'Sorry to disturb you. I've brought you some coffee.'

'Very considerate,' Bernie said, blinking at her sleepily. He looked at his watch. It was twenty past ten. He sat up abruptly and took the coffee.

DC Huxtable sat down close to him. 'You were right, sir,' she began in a mild Liverpudlian accent. 'We chased up Henry Ames's solicitor. He wasn't saying much, but Clive Bates did send him. In the meantime a couple of the jacks in the basement had another chat with our Henry. We got the address of this derelict off Kensington Park Road. We went round there. It was the right place, all right, but the buckos were gone.'

'Gone?' Bernie said. 'What about the girls?'

'Not there. That's the funny part,' DC Huxtable said, a shallow crease appearing between her eyes. 'There was no sign of them. Either we've got this wrong, or the girls aren't being kept in the same place at all. It's rather unusual.'

'Oh Lord,' Bernie said, pinching the bridge of his nose to goad his wits. 'What did you find then?'

'All sorts of bloody rubbish,' she said in frank disgust. 'Likely they'd been living off fish and chips and cold baked beans for days. That and Weetabix. But there was only the four beds and four sleeping-bags. If they were keeping prisoners there, they left no trace. And I can't believe that, because they left in a hurry when they went. There was this portable telly in there and it was still on.'

'Anything else?' Bernie sat holding his untouched coffee. He was deeply disappointed.

'Well, there was a cassette-recorder. We took that, of course. Then there was a plastic machine-gun and a cap-pistol. Oh, and it looks like one of them's a user. We found a syringe with a spoon and a candle.' She looked at Bernie with a touch of concern. 'Look, why don't you get off home, sir,' she said. 'We'll let you know the minute anything comes up.'

'Might as well,' Bernie said, getting stiffly to his feet.

'Thank you for stopping by with the news.' Outside, he yawned and stretched. He had one more errand to run before he could go home.

The cellar door crashing open seemed to be part of Anna's nightmare. A rough hand clamped over her mouth, and she found herself on her feet struggling and biting even before her eyes opened.

Verity cried out, a thin terrified scream, a sort of dream-scream where the larynx stays paralyzed, so shocked that she wet herself. Anna saw the widening stain as Verity was manhandled off the bed. Then Anna went down on the floor in a flurry of knees and elbows.

It was pointless. Close-quarter fighting with two men in crash helmets won nothing but bruises. She stopped struggling and was hauled to her feet. She saw that Verity now had a handkerchief tied across her mouth and another over her eyes. Rattle had one of her arms twisted behind her back. Roll was politely holding the other one.

Anna said, 'What the hell is going on?' It was the last thing she said for some time. Shake locked his arm around her throat and Lester forced a balled-up handkerchief into her open mouth. That'll teach me to keep it shut, Anna thought stupidly, and in an irrelevant flash of concern hoped the handkerchief was a clean one. Her stomach heaved. Lester said, 'I've been wanting to do that since the first time I saw you,' and tied something else around her mouth so that she couldn't spit the handkerchief out. 'Tie her up.' Everyone looked around and Anna could see quite clearly there was no rope.

'I left it in the van,' Roll said.

'You useless git,' Shake said savagely. 'This is the last time I work with you.'

Lester swore. 'Berk! You pissing berk. Give me your sodding bootlace then.'

Roll let go of Verity's arm and unlaced one of his boots.

Lester snatched the lace and tied Anna's thumbs together behind her back. Then they blindfolded her.

She was pushed, stumbling and falling, towards the door, cutting her bare feet on the broken glass as she went. Panic rose. She tried to breathe steadily through her nose, but fear worked unkindly on her sinuses and she couldn't seem to get enough air into her lungs. Her face ached in the cold way it does when you can't see and you're sure you're going to walk smack into a wall. She tried counting to calm herself. Eleven steps, turn left, then some stairs. Thirteen stairs. A door. Turn right. Fifty-four steps along something that echoed. Another door. Five steps. Another door. Fresh air and rain. Ninety-seven paces across something that felt like splitting asphalt. A thin splinter of glass lodged in the ball of her left foot. It pricked her at every step.

Then there was a wrenching metallic sound. Someone pushed at the back of her head so that she stooped. Then she was pushed forward again on to mud. Eight paces. Anna stopped counting and fell over. 'Get up!' Anna got up. They were picking their way over rough ground. No grass. Mud, concrete, bricks. Anna fell again. By the heaves, curses and scuffling, she guessed that Verity was falling regularly too. Her jeans tore over bruised knees. Her feet went numb with continuous scrapes and stubbings.

It was crazy, she thought, plain crazy. The circumstances did not merit such rough handling. And why were they walking such a long way? Someone would surely see and wonder at two girls being dragged along in the middle of the night.

They stumbled through another barrier, and at last Anna felt pavement beneath her feet. She heard car doors being opened and then, propelled by a shove from behind, she climbed into the back of a van. People scrambled over her as the van lurched off.

She couldn't keep the balled-up fabric away from the back of her throat and she was constantly on the verge of retching or choking on it. The smell of her own sweat sickened her too. She felt filthy, ill, and completely demoralized.

There was only one thing left she could attempt. She had to get the bootlace off her thumbs before they swelled and made it impossible. She rolled one thumb over the other and started pushing the lace down with her fingers. It was surprisingly easy. In a couple of minutes, her thumbs were free, and she sat crosslegged with her hands behind her back and waited, rocking with the motion of the van.

CHAPTER 26

Mrs Ames did not have a telephone and Bernie had promised Henry that he would go and see her. Now it was late, nearly midnight, and he wondered if she would still be up or if he would have to come back in the morning.

It started to rain weakly as he parked his car outside the house. It had rained on and off for nearly a month, he reflected, crossing the pavement; it was time to spray the roses again for mildew. A light shone from the basement, so he ignored the front door and went down the area steps, and rapped on the kitchen door.

The woman who opened the door was wearing a crimson quilted dressing-gown. Her grey hair was rolled up at the ends on pink plastic rollers and covered with a thick brown hairnet. She didn't look at all apprehensive of midnight visitors. Muscular hands were balled into ample fists on her wide hips.

'Fine time to come calling,' she said.

'I've got some news of your son, Henry,' Bernie said,

thinking that such a sturdy woman might have plenty of sons to choose from.

'Oh yes?' she said, chin out. 'Bit late, you are. They already sent a woman round. Are you a copper too?'

Bernie introduced himself.

'You're the one who ran him in, then?' she accused.

' 'Fraid so,' Bernie said. 'One of the missing women is a friend of mine.'

'Oh well, you did what you had to. Come in,' she said surprisingly. 'I was just having a brew before turning in.'

The kettle was whistling on a gas-stove that almost qualified as an antique. Mrs Ames made tea in a heavy brown pot and served it in thick willow-pattern cups. The kitchen smelled of pine disinfectant and Coal Tar soap. The smell of Poor But Proud was almost as potent.

'I'm sorry about the trouble your son's in,' Bernie began, taking his cup. The tea looked as strong as Mrs Ames did. He drank it gratefully.

'Oh well,' she said, sitting down opposite him. 'He's the only one as turned out a bit iffy. The youngest, you know. Maybe I spoiled him. He was a bit of an afterthought, just before my old Ed was took.' She did not look capable of spoiling anyone. 'I had hopes of him,' she continued. 'He's not daft, you know. Twenty years ago he'd've turned out all right.'

Bernie said, 'I know what you mean. These are funny old times.'

'I brought him up like the others,' she said, almost to herself. 'I've stood by him. But what can you do? He doesn't tell me what he's up to, so I can't even lie for him, can I?'

Bernie thought that was one of the saddest things a mother could say. He said, 'Never mind, Mrs Ames. He'll be home soon. I don't think they'll be too hard on him.'

'And that's another thing. Why shouldn't they be hard on him if he's done wrong? I don't mean him in particular, 'course I don't. But people are getting away with murder these days. When I was a kid, we got a good clip round the ear and we knew where we was. Not anymore. And are the kids any happier, I ask you? Not to my eyes, anyway.'

'No, well,' Bernie began, wanting to change the subject, 'a lot of things have changed for the better. You can't have everything.'

'It's the kids I'm talking about.' She was in full spate now. 'They grow up too fast and without enough sense to fill a mouse's ear. And with no one to tell them any different. Given up. That's what our generation's done.'

'It's not as bad as that, Mrs Ames,' Bernie said, getting up. He thought he'd better leave or she'd never stop.

'Take that old school over the wall there,' she went on, taking no notice. 'I went there. All my kids went there. Then they close it up and send all the kids to the Comprehensive. That's where Henry started to go wrong. They let them run around like a pack of wild animals. What's wrong with the old school? I used to know all the teachers there. Now it's just standing there empty, good for nothing. They've even got squatters in now. I phoned the Council but they don't want to know either.'

'Squatters?' Bernie said. 'In an old school?'

'I heard them shouting. I've heard them shouting for three days on and off. It must be one of those new religions.'

'Sunday,' Bernie said. 'Not before then? Are you sure?'

' 'Course I'm sure,' she said. 'I thought at the time, kids don't care who they disturb. People like a lie-in of a Sunday.'

'They do indeed,' Bernie said evenly. 'Well, Mrs Ames, I've got to be going now. Many thanks for the tea.'

The van jolted to a stop, throwing Anna on her side. The doors opened. There was a scuffle and a thump. The doors closed and they were off again, revving up to a high speed. Anna stayed down, trying to sense what had happened. She couldn't. A few minutes later they stopped again, and again the doors opened. Someone grabbed her ankles and dragged her across the metal floor. Her feet touched the ground and then she was pulled, running blind, first across tarmac and then grass. Someone pushed her heavily in the middle of the back and she was sent flying, head first, into a bush. She only just had time to protect her face with her arms and be grateful she had managed to untie her thumbs.

She hung, off balance in the bush, and listened until she heard the van accelerate away. Then, with fingers that trembled uncontrollably, she pulled the gag down over her chin and removed the sodden handkerchief from her mouth. Her throat felt like an empty cavern without it. She pulled off the blindfold and carefully extricated herself from the bush.

'It's over,' she said aloud. Suddenly her knees packed up and she sat down heavily on the wet grass. There was a knot of emotion deep in her belly and she felt that if it came unravelled she might weep.

Then she remembered Verity. They must have dropped Verity the first time the van stopped, somewhere not far away. She got up and looked around. Dark shapes of trees and shrubs loomed out of the night. She made for the road. The trouble was that she couldn't tell for sure which direction was back towards Verity. She didn't think she had crossed the road after leaving the van. But at the time she had been more concerned with her own balance than with topography. She decided, on the whole, that she hadn't crossed the road, so she turned right and walked on, calling Verity's name.

She wished she knew where she was. She wished for a pair of shoes and a warm coat. She wished Verity would answer. But as no fairy godmother popped out of the

gloom, she kept wishing and walking. Once she stopped
and tried to dig the glass out of the sole of her foot with
her fingernails, but it was too deeply embedded, so she
limped on with a growing sense of failure. In fact she felt
profound humiliation at her circumstances. She had been
hijacked by a bunch of half-wits who thought with the
seat of their pants if they thought at all. And she, the
'superior cow', hadn't been able to do a thing about it.
Now here she was, shoeless, witless, and lost. You
should've joined the Girl Guides when you had the
chance, she thought, it's about all you're fit for.

Detective-Inspector Chapple said, 'Everyone's in place
now. We might as well go in.' Bernie nodded and took his
hands out of his pockets. The constable used the bolt-
cutters on the chain that bound the iron gates and swung
them open.

'We're going in now,' Chapple said into his radio. 'I
hope to Christ you're right,' he muttered to Bernie as they
crossed the deserted playground. 'We'll look like right
nanas if you're wrong.'

Five men separated and circled the building. Bernie
and Chapple tried the main entrance. 'Door's been
forced,' Chapple said. The radio crackled. A remote
voice informed them, 'Window to the cellar broken on
the south side, sir.'

'All right, stay there,' Chapple replied. 'I am now
entering the building with Constable Knowles and Mr
Schiller.'

They pushed the main door open. Chapple switched
his torch on. They found themselves in a large porch with
a double row of coat-hooks on the walls. Another door
opened on to a long corridor.

'Someone's been here all right,' Chapple murmured.
'Look at all that dust. You know, I went to a school just

like this, in Streatham. They must've been laid by the same hen.'

They found the door to the basement. Chapple went down first. He moved very quietly and shielded the torch light with his fingers. Silently, they explored the boiler-room and storerooms.

'Here it is, sir,' Knowles said suddenly. 'Gawd, what a pong!'

Chapple found the light-switch and turned it on. Knowles said, 'Not exactly cosy, is it, sir?'

'I wouldn't call it home from home, no,' Chapple said. 'Well, this is it, I'd say. But too bloody late. I suppose we might find a few prints, etcetera. No good hanging around now. Are you coming, Mr Schiller?'

Bernie was surveying the room, taking in the bare tattered mattress, the paper-thin blankets, the pool of rainwater on the floor, the broken glass, the buckets.

'Are you coming, Mr Schiller?' Chapple repeated patiently.

'There's blood on the floor,' Bernie said stiffly.

CHAPTER 27

Anna looked through the double glass doors. Everything was quiet and clean, bright with flat fluorescent lighting. She pressed the bell. A constable came to the General Enquiries window, looked at her, and a buzzer sounded by the door. Anna went into the police station.

The desk was to her right, all neat and tidy. Drunk and Disorderly hour was long gone. She limped over. The desk-sergeant looked up from the *Anglers' Gazette* and said, 'Dear, dear, dear. Oh dearie me.' First impressions were important.

Anna said, 'My name is Anna Lee. I—'

'Just a minute,' the desk-sergeant interrupted. A smooth-faced constable of about twenty and a middle-aged man in a torn tweed coat came up from behind.

The constable said, 'I have arrested this man for breaking into a car in Steeple Road. The circumstances are . . .'

'I didn't break anything.'

Anna said, 'This is important.'

'Just a minute,' the sergeant said again. 'Go and sit down over there, I've got some particulars to take.' The particulars included name, address, place of work, telephone number, almost everything but hat-size.

Anna sat on a bench and waited. Nothing seemed real. Finally the constable took the man in the tweed coat away. Anna approached the desk again. The sergeant finished writing. He said, 'Would you mind rolling up your sleeves?' Anna knew she must look terrible, but she hadn't thought she looked as bad as all that. She said, 'Please, this is very important.'

'Just show me your arms, please,' the sergeant insisted politely. She rolled up her sleeves and displayed her arms.

'My name is Anna Lee. On Saturday I was kidnapped with another girl, Verity Hewit. Verity Ellen Hewit,' she said quickly while he examined her skin for needle marks. 'You must have some information about it.'

The sergeant said, 'Just a minute.' It seemed to be his favourite phrase. He riffled through some papers behind the desk. 'Anna Lee,' he said staring at her at last. 'Have you any identification, Miss Lee?'

Miss Lee. That was a step in the right direction, she thought, and rolled down her sleeves. She was shivering. She said, 'No, I dropped my bag outside Swiss Cottage swimming pool on Saturday when the incident occurred.' Being in a police station brought all the old jargon back. Anna went on to give all her own particulars.

He jotted, and checked everything she said with his

own information which he kept hidden behind his arm. She felt in the pockets of her jeans and shirt. On the desk in front of him, she placed the piece of cellophane, the shard of glass, and the faded cleaners' label.

'What's that?' he said, poking the cellophane with the rubber end of his pencil.

'I thought they might help with identification,' Anna said. Her tongue felt thick and she was having trouble arranging her thoughts. 'You see, I don't know who those yobs are, I never saw their faces, so I thought I might as well take their prints instead.'

'That's not evidence,' he said disdainfully.

'I know,' she said wearily. 'I just thought it might help, if you didn't already know who you were looking for.'

'As a matter of fact, we do,' he said, looking again at the papers behind his arm. 'There's four lads wanted for questioning in connection with your little episode. Still, you weren't to know that,' he added, softening. 'Give me a minute now. I've got some phoning to do to see if what you've told me isn't all my eye.' The bench drew Anna like a magnet. She felt as boneless as a cod fillet.

After a while he finished his call. 'Well, Anna,' he said. 'It's nice to see you. One of the lads'll take you down to an interview room. I'll get someone to make you a nice cup of tea.'

Anna nearly wept. Instead she said, 'Where are we? I'm afraid I've got no idea where I am.'

'Wimbledon,' the deskman said, surprised. 'You've been wandering about on Wimbledon Common.'

Anna followed the constable down a passage to the interview room: a small room with more strip lighting, a table, and three chairs. It was lined with insulating board and decorated with cream paint and a few crime prevention notices.

A WPC came in with a huge white mug of tea and a bowl of sugar on a tray. It was too hot to drink straight away. Anna clasped the mug in both hands to trap the warmth. The WPC said, 'You are in a state, aren't you?'

'A state of grace,' Anna said, beaming at the tea. 'You'll never know how good it looks.'

'Look at your poor feet,' the WPC said. 'I'll get something from the medical room.'

'Hot tea!' Anna sighed, taking her first mouthful and burning her tongue. 'I could die happy now.'

'Perhaps an aspirin too,' the WPC said worriedly, going out.

She came back after a while with a bowl of hot water, a first-aid kit, and a red stretcher blanket. She poured Dettol into the water and Anna soaked her feet, nestled into the blanket, and savoured the tea.

The WPC was a plump, fair woman called Joan. She picked the glass out of Anna's foot with a pair of tweezers and smeared the cuts with Savlon. 'I can't find a spare pair of shoes,' she said, 'but I think I can come up with some clean socks.'

'And some more tea?' Anna suggested hopefully. She didn't give a damn about her feet anymore. Joan went away, and Anna rested her head on her arms and went to sleep.

Joan shook her awake. 'Socks,' she said, 'and there's a car waiting to take you home.'

'No keys,' Anna mumbled, rubbing her eyes with grimy knuckles. 'I've lost the keys.'

'Haven't you got a neighbour you can wake up?'

'Oh yeah.' Anna put the socks on. 'Good old Selwyn. Beauty sleep never worked on him anyway.' Joan took the blanket and folded it neatly.

'Any news of Verity?' Anna asked the sergeant on her way past the desk.

'Nothing yet,' he said, 'but don't you worry. She'll turn up.' Anna didn't worry. It was someone else's turn to worry about Verity now. She slept all the way home in the car.

'Christ,' Selwyn said, when he opened the front door, blinking like a ruffled owl. 'You look like an extra from a Hammer film.'

'You're wonderful too,' Anna said wearily. She had waited a long time on the doorstep, nearly asleep on her feet. 'I need the spare key.'

'No, I mean, thank God you're all right.' He nearly tripped over his fraying dressing-gown cord in his haste to find the key. 'Where have you been? Everyone's been going potty. Christ! I nearly didn't answer the door. Bea's taken a pill, you see, and you never know at this time of night.'

'It's morning.'

'Is it? So it is.' Selwyn produced the key from under a thin pile of unpaid bills in a porcelain dish. 'What happened? Where have you been? How on earth did you get away?'

Anna took the key. She said, 'The answer to the second question is, I don't know. The other two will have to wait till later.'

'Oh come on, Leo,' Selwyn said, bright-eyed, as he followed her up the stairs. 'I'll never get back to sleep now.'

'Well, I will,' Anna said with absolute certainty.

'Tired?' Selwyn said, changing tack with the speed of lightning. He could be quite merciless when his curiosity was aroused. 'Look, I could make you a sandwich or something, while you have a bath. You do need a bath, don't you? You could shout through the bathroom door.'

'What would the neighbours say?'

'I *am* the bloody neighbours,' Selwyn cried. 'Don't be so mean, Leo. Don't keep me in suspense.'

'Look, Selwyn,' Anna said, opening her door. 'I'm so tired I could sleep on a coathanger. I stink like a skunk's

Y-fronts and if I have to answer any more questions tonight I'll wake up in the biscuit tin.'

'But it's morning,' Selwyn protested. 'You said so yourself.'

CHAPTER 28

Anna woke to the sound of plastic gutters crackling as they adjusted to the warm sunshine. She opened all the windows and grinned ironically. The sun seemed to mock her. Where were you when I needed you most? she thought, going to the bathroom and stripping off her filthy clothes. She flung them in a corner. When she had come in she had thrown herself on the bed just as she was, and dived into sleep as if it were a warm dark pool. Now she wished she had an open fire where she could burn the rancid things.

But first things first. She began by brushing her teeth. For days she had felt as if there were a fitted carpet in her mouth. So brushing, rinsing, spitting, and brushing again, she got rid of it. She showered, and washed her hair three times. Then she ran a deep bath, listening with pleasure to the water boiling through the Ascot. She soaked in it till her fingers took on the texture of pickled walnuts, thinking of nothing but the delight of a clean skin. She dried herself with a fresh towel, even though the one she had been using last week was still on the rail. She wrapped her wet hair with another. Nothing but the best, she promised herself. The clothes she chose to wear were white. Advertising, she thought sarcastically, but she felt weightless in them.

Selwyn knocked, and brought in a pint of milk and a face like a question mark. 'I heard the water running,' he said shamelessly. Anna sighed and put the receiver back

on the phone. Duty had to begin somewhere. It began almost immediately. The phone rang.

Beryl said, 'I've been trying to get hold of you since nine o'clock this morning. Have you any idea what time it is?'

'No,' Anna said, 'what time is it?'

'Ten past twelve. The Commander wants to see you.'

'When?'

'Three-thirty sharp.'

'Sharp,' Anna repeated. 'Thanks for calling, I've been ever so worried about you.'

'The police told us you were all right,' Beryl said tartly, 'and some of us have work to do.' She hung up, leaving Anna still searching for the last word.

She went to the kitchen and vented her frustration on an orange.

'I've been taking calls for you all morning,' Selwyn told her virtuously. 'Luckily for you, the first one was Bernie who said whatever happened not to wake you. So I didn't.'

'What a mensch,' Anna said. Orange juice had never tasted so pure and clean.

'It wasn't easy,' Selwyn said, misunderstanding. 'I must say you look terrific this morning,' he went on with an ingratiating smile. 'You smell better too.'

' "Je Reviens",' she told him, pleased. 'I'm celebrating. Coffee?'

'Just give me the story,' Selwyn pleaded, running out of artifice. 'I need coffee like I need six fingers. Tales of heroism, that's what I want.'

'Well, you'd better read a good book, then,' Anna said, filling the kettle. 'Heroism is right out of style in this story. I didn't even escape. We were dumped on Wimbledon Common like a couple of Christmas puppies.'

'Gagged and blindfolded?' Selwyn asked, with unfeigned hope.

'Yes, you can keep gagged and blindfolded.' Anna lit the gas and found some eggs in the fridge.

'Fantastic,' Selwyn said blissfully. ' "Learn to see by milky moonshine . . . And learn to hear the night-bird crying, heavy feathered, lonesome flying . . ." '

'What a load of old moolie,' Anna said in disgust. 'Or is that one of yours?'

' "Diana, watch the night-bird fly. And learn to do your killing silently," ' Selwyn quoted, too enthralled to be offended. 'It's an old one from when I was still drawn to the classics. Don't you see yourself as Diana the Huntress sometimes?'

'Not today, thanks,' Anna said, putting two eggs in to boil. The bread was stale, but it would do for toasting. 'In fact I don't see myself as anything unless there's a character in the classics who's the exact opposite of King Midas.'

The doorbell rang and Selwyn thundered downstairs. Bernie came in just as Anna was pouring coffee. 'All right?' he said casually, smiling so broadly it looked as if his face might split.

'Yes, thanks,' Anna said, reaching for another mug and giving as good as she got. His eyes looked slightly sunken, but otherwise he was just the same.

'We found where they'd kept you,' he said, accepting the coffee. 'I'd say about half an hour after you'd gone. Of course.' Selwyn hovered expectantly behind him, so Anna gave him a full mug too.

'Story of my life,' she said flippantly, passing the sugar. 'Where was it?'

'A disused school, off Kennington Road.'

'A school, huh? I thought it might be something institutional: all those bars and laminated glass.'

'I found your pick too,' Bernie said, stirring sugar into his coffee. 'Did it work?'

'Yes, well, it would've done, if those silly sods had ever

forgotten the bolts.'

'You can't win 'em all,' Bernie said cheerfully. 'Kept you busy though, didn't it?'

'What's happened to Verity?' Anna asked, guilt at last overcoming her pleasure in simple things.

'Oh, she's fine. A woman found her crying by the roadside, drove her home, and phoned her parents. She's right as rain.'

Anna busied herself taking eggs out of the boiling water. She gave it her full attention. Bernie said, 'Don't feel too bad about it. There wasn't a thing you could've done.'

'There should have been something.' She buttered the toast.

'Well, there wasn't. So don't torture yourself,' Bernie said kindly. 'Look, I've brought your handbag. And I found your sandals too.' He emptied his carrier bag on the kitchen table. 'I had a bit of a job persuading DI Chapple the sandals weren't evidence.'

'Just think: you actually found the place,' Selwyn said, unable to contain himself any longer. 'And when you found it there was nothing but a pathetic pair of sandals to tell the tale. What was it like?'

'Well, Mr Price,' Bernie began seriously, 'it was your average Gothic dungeon, deep in the bowels of the earth. Stone flags on the floor, the barred window curtained by the weaving of a million spiders.'

'Don't forget the bats,' Anna said, starting to eat her eggs, 'and the hunchback.'

'I'll give you bats!' Selwyn shouted furiously. 'You're both so bloody English. Why can't you tell a story properly instead of looking at it out of the corner of your eye. Hints, that's all I get. Leo, do you know, this man has been running himself ragged trying to find you. And all you can do is crack jokes about bats!'

'Of course she knows,' Bernie said soothingly. 'Now let's

just drink our coffee. And I'll tell you what I did.' He told his story simply, Anna filled in, and Selwyn stopped fidgeting.

'Good Lord,' he said, when Bernie got to the bit about Mrs Ames, 'you mean she actually called the Council about the shouting?'

'That's right,' Bernie said. 'When I was a lad, they'd've sent someone round straight away.'

'Nobody's that old,' Anna said. Bernie laughed.

Selwyn said, 'What about these blokes, what's happened to them?'

'Nothing yet. But it won't be long. They'll be coming out of the woodwork soon enough. Listen—'He turned to Anna. 'I've got to get back to the shop now. Want a lift?'

'No, thanks,' Anna said, 'not till I have to. What sort of a mood's Himself in, anyway?'

'Sunny intervals,' Bernie said, getting up. 'He's added this one to his clear-up rate, and it makes him look good.'

'A nod and a wink to the Met?'

'And very grateful they were too. Or so he says. Helped their clear-up rate as well. Personally, I think we owe a lot to Willy Dutch's amigos. They must've put the frighteners on Gary Natt's mob. I can't see him caving in for any other reason.' He laughed. 'But don't tell that to Himself when you see him. Good Solid Detection and don't you forget it.'

'GSD,' Anna said, giving him the thumbs up.

'Right. And you ought to get outside while the sun lasts. You've got a touch of the prison pales.'

When he had gone, Anna busied herself with the flat. She dusted and hoovered and played records, enjoying all the unimportant things that were now, in her mind, tributes to civilization. In fact, she dwelled lovingly on all the boring chores she usually skimped.

For a while Selwyn followed her around with probing questions, like a bad conscience. She did not want to choke him off, but she didn't want to answer him properly either, so she compromised with flippancy. This soon enraged him to the point where he stormed back downstairs shouting that the only people who knew how to tell a good story were the Celts, whereas she was only mongrel English who didn't even have a decent respect for curiosity.

Anna was sorry, but only a little. She knew she would have to think about it sometime. But not today. Today was for fresh air and open spaces. After a while she took Bernie's advice, as she usually did in the end, and went out.

She bought half a pound of black cherries and took them to Holland Park. Young mothers clutched their toddlers' cardigans and squinted suspiciously at the sun. They couldn't believe their luck.

Anna lay on her back in the grass behind the Commonwealth Centre, spitting out cherry stones, and couldn't believe it either. But it was just a part of English summertime: one day of happy warmth for every week of wishing you hadn't turned the central heating off in May.

CHAPTER 29

Brierly said, 'Good to see you, Miss Lee. I hope you are recovering from your experience.' The evening paper was open in front of him on his immaculate desk.

'I'm fine,' Anna said. 'Thank you.'

'Good. Excellent,' he said distractedly. 'Have you read this?' He pushed the newspaper across his desk. It was open at page two. Anna picked it up. A picture of Verity stared up at her. Verity, her face creased by a wide smile, was flanked by a balding middle-aged man on one side and a permed middle-aged woman on the other. They all

had their arms around each other and shared the same
self-conscious grin. The caption read, TOGETHER AGAIN.
A BRAVE LITTLE GIRL WINS THROUGH.

Anna grimaced. 'Little?' she said. 'She's bigger than I
am. She'll like this though.' She read on.

*A story that couldn't be told till now, because of police
fears for her safety: brave young Verity Hewit, aged
fourteen, was last night restored to her waiting parents
and tells of her ordeal. Said father, antique dealer
Roland Hewit, 'This is the best moment of my life. Her
mother and I are over the moon. We're so proud of our
little girl. She was terrified but kept her head.'*

*Verity was kidnapped a week ago for reasons yet to
be disclosed . . .*

'A week?' Anna said incredulously.

*Imprisoned in a bleak cellar room, little Verity had to
withstand the ravages of cold, fear and hunger. When
asked about her captors, Verity said, 'They weren't too
bad really. One was quite friendly. Some people just
don't deserve respect or good manners. But I don't bear
them a grudge.'*

'Blimey!' Anna said, and skipped a couple of
paragraphs. The last one said:

*Sharing little Verity's ordeal in captivity was Annie
Lease who, hearing Verity's cries for help, had a go and
went to her aid. Annie Lease is described as a librarian,
aged twenty-seven, from Brondesbury.*

'How do they do it?' Anna asked. 'Four facts in that last
sentence, and every one of them wrong. Is it a talent, or
do they have to work at it?'

'It is just conceivable,' Mr Brierly said, running his
forefinger delicately over one eyebrow, 'that in the remote
possibility interest in this story is maintained, someone
might get it right.' He paused, then added conversationally, 'I wouldn't want that to happen.'

'Nor would I,' Anna said with feeling.

'I thought not,' Brierly said. 'I'm so glad we are in agreement.' He folded the paper neatly and put it in the waste-paper basket.

'What did we do about Claire Fourie, in the end?' Anna said to change the subject.

'Hmmm, well, we sent her father a report, of course,' Brierly said with distaste. 'But nothing he could get his teeth into. The man was clearly unstable. Now, I expect you'd like tomorrow free to clear up your affairs.'

'Yes,' Anna said, surprised, 'yes, I would. Thank you.' It occurred to her that Mr Brierly was most pleased when she showed her weaknesses. It gave him great satisfaction to have his opinions about her incompetence confirmed. She was being rewarded for failure as she would never be rewarded for success. But she was not one to look a gift horse in the mouth, so she left quickly before he could change his mind.

She wasn't quick enough to escape Beryl though. Not many people were.

'You're late with your tea-money,' she said as Anna tried to slip unnoticed down the stairs.

'And you're late with my expenses,' Anna replied, paying up reluctantly.

'I can't read your writing,' Beryl countered, joyfully handing her a sheaf of receipts neatly pinned together at the corners, 'Would you mind doing them again? And by the way, there's a Chinaman wanting to speak to you urgently.'

They met in Kensington Gardens where the air was still, and people lay around on the grass as if they had been spread out to dry. The sun shone low in the sky, but starved Londoners wanted every last minute of it. Anna saw Gene coming from a long way off. He was wearing a blue T-shirt and his jacket was slung over one shoulder. England did not suit him, she thought, as he came closer.

Raincoats and thick jackets seemed to fetter him and make him smaller. What he needed was sun on his arms and summer clothes.

'Hey,' he said putting his arms around her and lifting her off her feet. 'You've lost weight.'

'They were very strict at the health farm,' she said, laughing. 'They wouldn't allow me a single cream bun.'

'I was worried sick about you,' he said without releasing her. 'How about a kiss, huh? You remember how to do that, don't you?'

'Yes,' Anna said in confusion, 'you just put your lips together and suck.'

'Oh, har-har,' he said, putting her down. 'OK then, tell all.'

'I'd rather not.' She took his hand and led him off in the direction of the Serpentine. His hand was hot and dry, and his skin smelled of newly cut grass. 'I really don't want to think about it yet. Let's just walk in the park and forget all about it for a while.'

'That bad, was it?'

'As disasters go, I'd put it in the bottom ten.'

The Serpentine was opaque with algae, and they watched a few lazy geese hanging motionless in the green water. Gene said, 'You don't look too well, you know. What you need is early nights and a lot of good food.'

'Sound advice,' Anna said. 'Your place?'

'As a matter of fact,' he said slowly, 'I'm all tied up tonight. I wish you'd rung me earlier. I don't like letting you down.' He kept his eyes on the water.

Anna said, 'Never mind. No need to feel badly.'

'I wish you had come to Weymouth,' he said idly. Anna stared at him.

'That was a pretty big mistake,' she said lightly.

'There's something maybe I ought to tell you,' he said hesitantly.

'Don't!' she said. 'I've had a basinful of somethings.

Any more could sink the ship. I'll take your advice, though. I'll eat well and sleep long, and then I'll phone you when I'm feeling stronger.'

'Yes,' he said, 'you do that. Probably I'll have everything straightened out by then.' He was going to say something else, but stopped himself. Anna was grateful. That evening she wanted to avoid even the thought of anything unpleasant. If it was bad news, it was her own fault anyway; she had refused to spend the weekend with him, she had consistently put her work first when there was any choice to be made, and she had kept him at a comfortable distance. If something exciting had cropped up for him in Weymouth it was too late to bitch about it now.

They walked together to Bayswater Road. The parting was friendly but a little uneasy.

'Take good care of yourself,' he said regretfully, 'and be sure to call me when you've got your muscles back, OK?' But Anna, walking home, felt that perhaps it was time for new beginnings. It wasn't right, she thought, to spend time on something she couldn't be wholehearted about. But even the crimson sky looked rather sorrowful.

CHAPTER 30

Anna dreamed she had a baby. It was so small that she put it in her pocket for safe-keeping while she went on a journey. After a while she put her hand in her pocket and found only fluff. The baby was gone. In a panic, she rushed around searching for it. At last she found it on a park bench. The night was dark, frosty, and wet. The baby was naked. It was lying as still as a stone, looking blue in the moonlight, and she knew she had let it die.

She woke up with a crushing sense of failure, and before

making coffee for breakfast, she rang the Hewits' number. Mrs Hewit answered the phone.

'Good heavens,' she said, when Anna told her who she was, 'I've been trying to get hold of you, but no one could tell me your number. My husband and I want to thank you for what you tried to do for our daughter.'

'That's all right, Mrs Hewit,' Anna said. 'I wish it could have been more. I just wanted to see if Verity was OK.'

'Oh, she's fine now,' Mrs Hewit said cheerfully. 'You know, a good sleep and some good nourishing food. Teenagers bounce right back.'

'I hope so. I was just wondering, well, she was very frightened, you know, and I was wondering if I could have a word with her?'

'I'm very grateful for your concern.' Mrs Hewit's voice changed subtly. She sounded embarrassed. 'But I honestly think it'd be better for her to forget all about it now.'

'I suppose you're right,' Anna said awkwardly. 'But I was thinking. You see, I don't think she ever understood what was going on in there. I think she felt squeezed between those lads and me. It was rough on her.'

'Oh, I'm sure she understood,' Mrs Hewit said quickly.

'Well, if she ever wants to talk to me about it, I'll give you my number.'

'No, really, that won't be necessary,' Mrs Hewit said decidedly. 'I know she'd prefer to forget the whole episode. I'm very grateful, truly I am, but you know young girls are very strange sometimes.'

'OK,' Anna said as lightly as she could. They said goodbye politely and Anna rang off. She shrugged, and made the coffee very strong. While she was drinking it, she phoned Mr Minh.

He said, 'You been away, Miss Lee? I can't find you anywhere. You sound sick. You sick or something?'

'No. No, I'm fine, Mr Minh.'

'Good. Good,' he said sadly. 'You be sick now, I think. You know engine hoist?'

'What happened, Mr Minh?' Anna said fatalistically.

'Chain break when we swap engine. So very sorry. Awful, lousy mess I think.'

'Oh Lord. Is there anything we can do?'

'Impossible,' Mr Minh said firmly. 'Some parts, OK. But no motor-car. Tell you what . . .'

'What?'

'You know Renault?' he said encouragingly. 'I talk to man.'

'You mean you will talk to him or you have talked to him?'

'I talk to man yesterday.' Mr Minh sounded surprised at her stupidity. 'I think we do a deal.'

'A deal?' Anna said suspiciously.

'Good deal. Same price, you keep Renault.' He sounded triumphant.

'Plus MOT?'

'OK.' He agreed much too smartly, Anna thought. She would probably find out why soon enough. 'What about the Triumph? Will you buy it for spares?'

'Not buy, sorry,' Mr Minh said. 'You take away anytime. Welcome.'

'OK. OK,' Anna said, defeated. 'You keep the spares. But I want a free service on the Renault as well as the MOT.'

'Good. Done.' Mr Minh said. He sounded as if he was having a fine morning.

Anna had left the Renault up in Belsize Park on Saturday. It was another lovely morning, and she would have gone straight out to collect the car, but a brace of policemen arrived to take her statement. They were very thorough so she was not free to leave the flat till after lunch. She asked if any arrests had been made. They hadn't, but someone thought they had seen Eric Tozer in

Brixton. The police thought that the other three were still in London too. It was just a matter of time, they said. They could afford to wait.

She caught a 31 bus to Swiss Cottage and walked from there, enjoying the sun and exercise and wanting to spend as much time out of doors as possible. She wanted to do something special to make up for lost time.

In the end, for want of a better idea, she went into a shop and bought an illustrated book about Alfred Hitchcock and a Big Bill Broonzy record. She had wanted them both for a long time and now she wouldn't put the purchase off any longer. In the same mood, she licked her lips over a display of ripe avocados and mangoes and bought some of each.

The Renault was parked in the street where the Fouries lived, about fifty yards from their house. As she passed, she saw a man sitting in a Fiat, reading the *Express*. She slowed her walk and saw, on the seat beside him, an open notebook, field glasses, and a camera.

She walked on and put her gifts to herself in the Renault. She opened all the car windows to let out the trapped heat and stood, waiting for the car to cool, looking back at the Fouries' house, weighing up pros and cons. Her old rainhat was on the back seat. She put it on and jammed it well down over her face. It would look ridiculous in this weather, but that was better than having mad Mr Fourie recognize her photograph. She locked the car again, walked quickly back to No. 29 and rang Janet Fourie's bell. The blue door she had watched so hard for so many days opened. Quickly she said, 'My name's Anna. I'm a friend of Verity's. May I come in?'

Janet Fourie hesitated for only a second. Then she swung the door wide and said, 'Gracious! You're the one . . . of course, come in, do.'

All the windows were open to catch the afternoon breeze, but even so the flat was warm. Janet Fourie was wearing a flowery cotton dress. She was bare-legged and barefoot. Her blonde hair was gathered loosely at the back of her neck. You could see she was Claire's mother, Anna thought, although the fine skin was lightly lined, and a lot of what was curved in Claire was hollowed in her mother.

'I met your friend, John Crocker, when he came to talk to Claire about the day at the swimming pool,' Mrs Fourie said. 'He was very upset about you, of course. What a nice man.'

'Yes,' Anna agreed. 'Although he's more a colleague than a friend.' She decided to take the bull by the horns. 'Did you know that he is a private detective and so am I?'

'You're joking,' Mrs Fourie said uncertainly.

'Well, if you think that's funny, wait till you hear this: there's another one in a black Fiat watching this house now. Where's Claire?'

'She went out with some friends,' Mrs Fourie said, confused.

'I'll bet a pound to a pear-drop there's someone else following her.'

'Why? What does all this mean?'

'Your ex-husband wants custody of Claire, Mrs Fourie. He employed the firm I work for to find evidence that you are an unfit mother. My boss thought he was unstable and refused to work for him after a week.'

'Then who is out there now?' Mrs Fourie went over to the window and peered through the net curtains. 'I can see him. He's reading a paper.'

'That's right,' Anna said. 'I don't know who he is, but it means that Claire's father hasn't given up.'

'But this is crazy,' Mrs Fourie said, sitting down.

'Yes,' Anna agreed and sat down too. 'I don't want to be rude, but I think Claire's father is off his trolley. I thought you ought to be warned, that's all.'

'Yes, yes, I see.' Janet Fourie rubbed her arms as if she

were cold. 'Thank you very much for telling me.' She was too nice, Anna thought, to criticize her ex-husband, even now.

She said, 'I'm afraid there's something else. There is evidence, you know, that you aren't keeping a proper eye on Claire. I collected some of it myself.'

'What do you mean?' Mrs Fourie said, startled. 'We lead a perfectly normal life here. In fact, I'd say it was almost boring.'

'I don't want to hurt you,' Anna said slowly, 'but I took photographs of Claire on Parliament Hill. She was smoking and drinking and taking drugs. We didn't give the photos to her father. But someone else could take another set and they might not give a damn about how sane he is.'

'Hold on a second,' Mrs Fourie said in a stunned voice. 'Give me a minute to think.' She jumped up and crossed distractedly to the window, looking out and rubbing her arms nervously. When she turned back, her face was calm. She asked, 'What else do you know? You might as well tell me everything.'

'Well, I don't know if the next bit is true or not,' Anna said cautiously, 'but, as you know, I was close to Verity for a few days. And Verity said that Claire was sleeping with a young squatter who lived in your basement.'

'I didn't know there was anyone downstairs.'

'Well, there was. He thought she was eighteen years old. On top of that, he was involved in Verity's kidnapping.'

'Oh dear,' she said, making a helpless gesture with her hands. 'This is very bad indeed.'

'I don't know,' Anna said truthfully, 'but I think it would be better to deal with it right now, and not wait till her father finds out. If he gets the evidence he wants, evidence of what I've told you, you'll never get the chance to sort her out.'

'No, I can see that. This is awful. I've brought Claire up on my own for a long time, and now she's nearly grown up, I thought we were over the worst.'

'It can't have been easy.'

'No. It's been very lonely,' she said, 'but I was always looking forward to a time when I could be Claire's friend, not just her mother. Maybe that's why I've encouraged her to have a life of her own. Something we could talk about, as equals.'

'Did she talk about it?' Anna asked.

'No. Now I come to think of it, she was always evading me,' Mrs Fourie admitted. 'I did most of the talking. Perhaps I have to go on being a mother till Claire lets me stop.'

'I'm not sure you can do anything else,' Anna said thoughtfully, 'although I know I can't blame you for wanting a companion rather than a dependant. When I was with Verity, I felt as if she'd put me in a box marked "Adult" to be leaned on at will, and there was nothing I could do or say to make her change her attitude. It got to be very wearing.'

'I'm very glad you came here,' Janet Fourie said, smiling suddenly. Her face looked young and hopeful. 'And I'm glad you blew the whistle on Claire. It's a shock of course, but it's the best thing that could have happened in the long run.'

'Well, that's a relief!' Anna said, getting up to go. 'I'd thought of a lot of things you could have said, and none of them was as nice as that.' She put her hat back on and thought of something else. She said awkwardly, 'I'd be even more relieved if you didn't tell anyone I came. This sort of conversation just isn't the done thing in my trade. I could lose my job.'

Mrs Fourie promised and they parted warmly, but Anna did not look back as she drove away. She felt she had been thoroughly unprofessional, but at least she had

made some attempt to redeem Claire. Her failure with
Verity still hurt; there was nothing to be done about that.
But with a much lighter heart she set out to find a chicken
tikka and some live music.